"Cover your [obscured]

Matt hit seve[obscured]with short blasts o[obscured]

Coughing, he wedged his shoulder under the edge of the counter and levered it up a few inches. "Go!" He had to bite back a groan when something ripped low down in his left side, where the scar tissue was thick and uncompromising.

"I'm out!" Gigi dragged herself up, clutching something to her chest.

"Come on!" They staggered toward the window. He boosted her out first. "Run. I'm right behind you."

Of course she didn't go anywhere, damn her, just turned back and reached for him as he came through. Not willing to take any more chances with her, he caught her by the waist, slung her over his shoulder and headed away from the fire.

JESSICA ANDERSEN

BEAR CLAW CONSPIRACY

TORONTO NEW YORK LONDON
AMSTERDAM PARIS SYDNEY HAMBURG
STOCKHOLM ATHENS TOKYO MILAN MADRID
PRAGUE WARSAW BUDAPEST AUCKLAND

Recycling programs
for this product may
not exist in your area.

ISBN-13: 978-0-373-69547-8

BEAR CLAW CONSPIRACY

Copyright © 2011 by Dr. Jessica S. Andersen

ABOUT THE AUTHOR

Jessica Andersen has worked as a geneticist, scientific editor, animal trainer and landscaper...but she's happiest when she's combining all of her many interests into writing romantic adventures that always have a twist of the unusual to them. Born and raised in the Boston area (Go, Sox!), Jessica can usually be found somewhere in New England, hard at work on her next happily ever after. For more on Jessica and her books, please check out www.JessicaAndersen.com and www.JessicaAndersenIntrigues.com.

Books by Jessica Andersen

*Bear Claw Creek Crime Lab

CAST OF CHARACTERS

Matt Blackthorn—This half-Cherokee park ranger is far more than he seems. But with wildfires threatening and criminals stalking his people, his wilderness peace is disrupted even before the arrival of a city-slicker CSI.

Gigi Lynd—A lovely crime scene analyst with big ambitions, Gigi doesn't have time for a serious relationship…especially not with a hunky yet complicated man like Matt. But when her work puts her in the line of fire, forcing them to team up, "complicated" doesn't even begin to describe it!

Percy Proudfoot—The mayor of Bear Claw Creek has put the city deeply in debt.

Tanya Dawes—Why was she out of her normal ranger territory when she was attacked?

Alex MacDonald—This local thug is up to no good… but he's clearly not working alone.

Tucker and Alyssa McDermott—The homicide detective and his very pregnant CSI wife are determined to help Matt and Gigi get to the bottom of things.

Jerry Osage—Maybe the death of this former assistant at the Bear Claw medical examiner's office isn't as cold of a case as it seems!

Chapter One

"Help! Help... She's... I need help!"

The shout came from outside Ranger Station Fourteen, followed seconds later by the sound of someone running flat out, skidding on the loose gravel of the trailhead.

Matt Blackthorn bit off his briefing mid-sentence and strode from his office, his pulse kicking and then leveling off as he went into crisis mode: six feet and two inches worth of black-haired, green-eyed competence, laced with the determination of his part-Cherokee forebears and the killer instincts that had once been his trademark.

Grizzled park service veteran Bert Grainger was right behind him, while young charmer Jim Feeney veered off to put the dispatcher on standby in case they needed outside help. The station's fourth ranger, a clever brunette named Tanya Dawes, was already out in the field. Hopefully, they wouldn't need her.

As Matt headed through the station's front room, he mentally reviewed the hikers who'd checked in at Station Fourteen—the most remote and isolated of the Bear Claw Canyon ranger stations—over the past few days. He fixed on the newlyweds who had come through earlier that morning. They had been too busy mooning over each other—and their new city-bought hiking gear—to really pay attention to his spiel on backcountry safety precautions.

Muttering a curse, he stiff-armed the door leading outside. *Damn it, I told them to head back down toward Bear Claw.* Station Three, with its brightly marked trails and pre-planned walking tour, would've been a better fit for those two. Fourteen was no place for city softies.

They hadn't listened, though. And sure enough, Mr. Newlywed—Cockleburr? Cockson? It was cock-something, anyway—was pelting toward him across the dirt parking lot, eyes frantic enough to have Matt's gut twisting.

"Oh, thank God you're here." Newlywed's words tumbled over each other as he staggered to a halt and sucked in a ragged breath. "She's hurt, unconscious, and—"

"Stop!" Matt said firmly, using his cut-through-the-panic voice. When Cochran—that was it, Cochran—quit babbling, Matt said, "What happened to your wife? Did she fall?" The trails were dry as hell and starting to crumble in places.

But Cochran shook his head furiously. "Tracy's fine. The woman we found is one of yours."

"One of—" Matt's stomach did a nosedive. "A *ranger?*"

Cochran patted his chest, near where the men and women who oversaw Bear Claw Canyon State Park wore their badgelike name tags. "Tanya. Her name's Tanya."

"Jim!" Bert bellowed back toward the station. "Get out here!"

"That's—" *Impossible,* Matt started to say, but then bit off the word. Arguing was a waste of time.

His mind locked on Tanya as he'd seen her last— pretending to ignore pretty-boy Jim while blowing a kiss to divorced, old-enough-to-be-her-father Bert as she headed out to one of the Jeeps. Her dark hair had been tied back, her dark eyes laughing as she had joked with the two men: one her self-proclaimed partner in meaningless flirtation, the other her friend.

Matt hadn't been part of the bunkhouse horseplay that morning or any other time. He had his own place beyond the station house and kept to himself. But Tanya was definitely one of his.

His ranger. His responsibility.

There was a commotion behind him as Jim thudded down the steps and Bert relayed the bad news. Jim blanched and surged forward, but Bert grabbed him by the arm and held him in check.

Matt focused on Cochran. His mind raced through scenarios from fixable to fatal. *Please let it be fixable.* "Where is she?"

Cochran gestured northward. "At the bottom of a shallow wash, that way, about forty-five, fifty minutes from here. We saw her when we were hiking up to this cave mouth that's shaped like a heart."

"That's right by Candle Rock!" Bert burst out. The distinctive formation was part of his patrol area, not Tanya's.

Matt bit off a curse. Candle Rock was difficult to reach, with too many river crossings for vehicles to get all the way in. And what the hell was Tanya doing over by Candle Rock? *Later,* he told himself. He'd worry about the whys later. "She's unconscious?"

Cochran nodded. "Looks like she slipped and fell. She had a knot on her head. There was a little blood, and she was cool to the touch, but her breathing and pulse both seemed steady. Trace stayed to try and warm her up."

"Good," Matt said gruffly. "Okay, then." He was starting to think the Cochrans weren't as much of a lost cause as he had initially pegged them for. And for Tanya's sake, he hoped to hell that was the case.

He turned to Jim. "Get an emergency medical chopper en route. Bert and I are going to drive in as far as we can and hike the rest of the way. We should get there about the same time as the chopper. I want you back here coordinating things."

Jim's face clouded. "But—"

"I could stay—" Bert began.

"Not open for discussion," Matt broke in. He gestured to Bert. "Get one of the first-aid duffels and our climbing gear." To Jim, he said in a low voice, "Let us take this one. You can see her later." When the kid—okay, he was twenty-five, but as far as Matt was concerned, still very much a kid—started to protest, Matt fixed him with a look. "That's an order."

Jim hesitated, then nodded reluctantly. They both knew that although Matt didn't pull rank often, he meant it when he did.

And in this case, he meant it in spades. He knew all too well that there was no room for emotion during a crisis…and when things went bad out in the backcountry, they could go very, very bad.

Tanya was an expert climber, though. What the hell had happened? And why was she out of her territory? Those questions clouded his concern for the young ranger as he drove his Jeep out toward Candle Rock, with Bert and Cochran following in a second vehicle.

Despite the rangers' best efforts to educate the hikers who had the chops to handle the backcountry and discourage the ones who didn't, the treacherous terrain, wildfires, poisonous snakes, and drought-starved predators had combined to take their toll. In his almost six years as head of Station Fourteen, he had led eight search parties and arranged transport of three bodies. His sector—which included the park's most remote territory—averaged an airlift a month, and two or three times that many hikers had to be driven straight to the E.R. Do not pass go. Do not collect two hundred dollars.

He hoped to hell this would be one of the easy ones, requiring little more than a couple of ibuprofen and a day or two off. If Tanya had been unconscious for an extended period, though, that didn't seem likely.

At the thought, he hit the gas and sent the Jeep lunging forward. Then, when the wheels shuddered, he made himself ease up and breathe. Panic didn't solve anything.

They made it most of the way to Candle Rock in the vehicles after all—the drought that had contributed to the wildfires currently devastating Sectors Five and Six was a backhanded blessing now, drying up the two rivers that usually blocked the route.

When their luck ran out at the base of a steep hill, they parked, shouldered their gear, and hiked in the rest of the way, jogging along a narrow game trail that crested a rocky, tree-lined ridge near the cave.

Matt brought up the rear, carrying his shotgun. If Tanya was bleeding, there would be scavengers in the area, maybe even one or more of the bigger predators.

"Up here!" Cochran ran forward, cresting the ridge as he called, "Trace? We're back!"

"Hurry!" a woman's voice responded immediately. "She's in shock, and I don't like how low her heart rate is getting."

Matt cursed and lunged up the last stretch and down the other side, partly jumping from one rock to another, partly skidding along the loose, crumbling gravel. "Get the ropes anchored," he said to Bert, waving the older man back as he reached the edge of the deep wash.

"Will do. You should wait until—"

"No time." Matt yanked the straps of his knapsack tighter, checked his shotgun, and jumped over the edge of the wash right behind Cochran.

He dropped nearly a dozen feet and his boots hit the ground hard, but he barely noticed the impact; his focus was locked on where Cochran had one arm around his wife. Their heads were tipped together, their bodies leaning into each other.

But even as that image burned itself inexplicably into Matt's brain, he looked past them where Tanya lay sprawled in the gravel. She was covered with two brightly colored jackets, and other pieces of the Cochrans' clothing were tucked around her. Her eyes were closed and a slender blood trail tracked across her cheek. Her supposedly shockproof radio lay smashed nearby, in a scuffed spot below the crumbled ledge.

Something jarred faintly wrong, but that was quickly blotted out by a twist of guilt. She looked so damn young lying there…and he had sent her out alone. Which was protocol, but still.

"Hey, Tanya," he said as he crouched down beside her. "It's Matt." Had she ever called him by his first name? He couldn't remember. "Bert's here, too. We're going to get you out of here."

Her pupils were unequal, her vitals too damn low across the board. Yeah, she was shocky all right. Concussed, too, and maybe suffering from internal injuries. It wasn't that much of a fall, but she must have landed exactly wrong.

Grabbing the radio off his belt, he toggled it to send. "Jim?"

There was a hiss and a squawk. "Did you find her?"

"Got her. How are we doing on that chopper?"

"Should be there any minute. How is she?"

"Banged up." The faint noise of rotor-thwack saved him from having to elaborate. "Chopper's here. Patch me through will you?"

As he was talking options with the pilot, a trio of climbing ropes sailed over the edge and slithered down, followed moments later by Bert. Raising his voice over the increasing noise of the helicopter, the grizzled ranger called, "They going to stay in the air and drop a basket?"

Matt shook his head. "The pilot thinks she can land on that flat section beyond the wash. We'll use the ropes to bring Tanya up and out." It felt good to have a plan, better to know she would soon be getting the medical help she needed. Turning back to the injured ranger, he gentled his voice and said, "The chopper's almost here. They'll get you down to the city, and—" He broke off when her eyelids fluttered. "Tanya? Can you hear me?"

She shifted uncomfortably and frowned, then lashed out with a fisted hand as though trying to physically fight off unconsciousness. Cochran and his wife made soothing noises but stayed back, yielding to Matt. He caught her flailing fist. "Easy, killer. You fell off the ledge and banged yourself up a bit, but the med techs are on their way."

Her lips moved. "Didn't…fall."

He blew out a relieved breath that she was making sense. "You hit your head. It'll come back." Maybe. Maybe not. At least she was talking.

But she shook her head, wincing at the pain brought by the move. "No fall. Ambushed."

His blood chilled, but it didn't make any sense. Ambushes were for narrow alleys and drug dealers, not wide-open skies and park rangers. Hallucination? Maybe. He didn't know. Leaning closer, he said urgently, "What happened?"

Her eyes opened to slits as she tried to focus on him. "Two men grabbed me…wanted…" She struggled to say something more, but then her body went lax as she lost her brief grip on consciousness.

"Wait!" He surged up onto his knees and bent over her, gripping her fisted hand in his. "What men?" The controlled crisis mode he'd long ago perfected lost out to anger at the thought of someone doing this to one of his people, on his territory, his watch. "Tanya, *what men?*"

"Matt." Bert gripped his shoulder. "She's out."

Damn it. He subsided, loosening his grip on her hand. When he did, something fell free and floated to the ground.

Cochran leaned in. "What's that?"

Catching the small, colorful scrap between his thumb and forefinger, Matt lifted it. "A feather."

The shaft was thin and curved, and the barbs ran a wild-colored gamut from white-and-black at the top to a deep reddish orange in the middle, then back to black at the base. He frowned at it, but there was no time to really get a good look, because right then the rotor noise increased to a roar and the chopper appeared overhead.

It paused, spun, and then dropped in for a more-haste-than-grace landing. Moments later, shouts and the sound of thudding footfalls up above announced the arrival of the med team.

Matt stuck the feather in his breast pocket and buttoned it in for safekeeping.

The next few minutes were ordered chaos as the medical team rappelled down and hustled to get Tanya stabilized for transport, with a rapid yet thorough triage, warming blankets and an IV line of fluids to combat the shock. The techs didn't say it, but he could see from their faces that they didn't like her continued unconsciousness any more than he did. Working quickly and efficiently, they strapped her down and okayed her for travel.

Working together, Matt, Bert, the Cochrans and the

med team hauled her out of the wash and loaded her onto the chopper.

Matt heard the copilot radioing ahead to let the hospital know they had a serious head injury on the way. He wanted somebody to look at her and say that she'd be fine, but it didn't happen.

He slid the door closed, then ducked out of range as the rotors screamed and the chopper lifted up and away, heading for the city. He was relieved to have Tanya in the care of professionals, but there wasn't any time to stand around congratulating himself on a job well done…especially when he hadn't done his job well at all.

It was his responsibility to make Sector Fourteen as safe as he possibly could. His mind churned. Two men, she had said. What men? What had happened, and why was she out of her normal range? Had she followed them and been discovered, or had they brought her all this way and dumped her? And what was the deal with the feather? Was it important, or just something she'd been carrying when she was ambushed?

He winced as phantom pain sliced through his lower left abdomen, where a gnarled scar and low-grade ulcer formed a pointed reminder that it wasn't his job to be asking those questions. Hadn't been for a long time.

As the rotor noise dimmed, he pulled Bert aside, out of the Cochrans' earshot. "Take those two back to the station and keep them there."

The other man darted a look at the hikers. "You think they hurt Tanya?"

"No. But they may have seen something and not even realized it."

Bert craned around, eyes widening as he followed Matt's thought process. "You think the guys who got Tanya are still around?"

Probably, said Matt's instincts. "Just get back to the station and put them in separate rooms so they can't compare stories any more than they already have. Then you can relieve Jim on the radio so he can go to the hospital. If he balks, make it an order."

He didn't think the younger man would give even a token protest. Jim and Tanya had been circling around each other for the past six months, ever since she transferred up from Station Seven, and the fear and emotion in the younger man's face had been real. While that kind of romantic connection didn't work for Matt, he wasn't about to make the choice for someone else. He had sworn off trying to run other people's lives.

"Aren't you coming back with us?" Bert asked, still looking around, searching for monsters in the shadows. But that was the thing about monsters. Most of the time, you couldn't see them until the damage was already done.

"I'm going to stay and look around, scare off any scavengers who might be interested in the scene." Human or otherwise. Matt tapped the butt of the shotgun riding over his shoulder. "I'll be fine."

Bert looked unconvinced, but there was enough of an enlisted man still left in him that he followed orders without further argument, collecting the Cochrans and getting them moving back toward the Jeeps.

When they were gone, Matt was left alone beneath a brilliantly blue sky, warmed by the summer sun. But the beauty and isolation didn't settle him like they normally did. Instead, there was a heavy weight on his chest as he lifted his radio. "Jim, you reading me?"

"Here, boss. She get away okay?"

"Yeah. They're en route. You can go down to the city as soon as Bert gets there. Right now, though, I need you to patch me through to Tucker McDermott." This wasn't a case for Homicide, really, but Tucker was a friend. One of his very few.

There was a beat of silence. "I thought she fell."

"It looks like it wasn't an accident."

"What?"

"Just put me through to Tucker, okay? Bert will fill you in when he gets there."

The patch-through from radio to telephone took a minute, but was necessary. There was no cell coverage in the back of beyond, and even satellite phones were hit-or-miss. So the rangers often relied on radios, especially for the more out-of-the-way sectors: Seven and Eight on the eastern side, Thirteen and Fourteen on the western side, and good old Sector Nine, which formed the bridge between the two lobes of the huge park… where the crime usually ran to vandalism and careless fires, not attempted murder.

Matt took a long look at the scuffed-up sidewall of the gulley and the three ropes that snaked from a big boulder and disappeared over the edge. He didn't need to glance down there to know that the bottom of the wash was churned up and littered with scraps from the med techs' sterile packaging. The scene was seriously contaminated, and it was going to take a hell of an analyst to make anything out of it. Fortunately, the Bear Claw P.D.'s crime lab was staffed by a group of

talented analysts who were the ultimate professionals…
with one glaring, purple-booted, on-loan-from-Denver
exception.

Matt grimaced at the intrusive image of sparkling
gray eyes in a sharp face framed by sleek dark hair. Gigi
Lynd. Even her name sounded expensive and citified, not
like anything that belonged out in the backcountry.

He would tell Tucker to send anyone but her. Hell,
Station Two's nature trail would be a stretch for someone like her…and the last thing he needed to be doing
right now was babysitting some city-slicker analyst who
dressed like she was looking for trouble.

Chapter Two

Gigi nailed three bad-guy targets, skipped the little old lady cutout, tagged the last two baddies and slapped her Beretta on the counter with a flourish that might not have been strictly necessary, but damn, she was on a roll.

Granted, the firing range's offerings were pretty basic, but still.

She slipped off her headphones and turned, just catching the tail end of her friend Alyssa's impressed whistle. The heavily pregnant blonde's eyes glittered with appreciation behind her tinted safety glasses, but she faked a pained look. "Please tell me you didn't just pick that up for the test, like you did the computer stuff you showed me."

Gigi grinned and slicked her dark, asymmetrically bobbed hair behind her ears before pulling her clip, clearing the chamber, and giving the weapon a quick, practiced wipe down. "I shot my first rifle when I was nine, started with handguns when I was thirteen."

"Thank God. I was starting to get seriously depressed, thinking that you'd only been shooting for the past six months or so."

"Nope. More like the past two decades. And you don't look the slightest bit depressed." In fact, the head of the Bear Claw P.D.'s Forensics Division looked amazing— rosy cheeked and curvy, with the mysterious "I know something you don't" look that Gigi associated with her sisters' first pregnancies. "I take it you're feeling better?"

"Incredible." Alyssa smoothed her palm across the top of her protruding belly. "After the past three weeks of abject almost-time-to-pop yuckiness, I woke up this morning feeling amazing." A smile touched her lips with an entirely different sort of knowing look. "Tucker did, too, much to his surprise and delight."

"Ouch." Gigi exaggerated the wince. "Taunting the celibate again, are we?"

Alyssa twinkled at her. "A girl who looks like you and shoots like that doesn't need to be celibate."

"Right. Because guys perform best at gunpoint." When Alyssa gave her a "yeah, right" look, Gigi lifted a shoulder. "I guess I'm not a casual sex kind of girl."

Her friend's blue eyes narrowed. "I never thought you were."

Maybe not, but plenty of guys looked at the outside packaging and thought they knew what was going on inside it. If she mentioned that, though, Alyssa would bring up the *m* word again—makeover—and that wasn't happening. What might look a little too glittery in Bear Claw played just fine in Denver, and Gigi liked her personal style. There was nothing wrong with being different.

So as they crossed the parking lot toward her borrowed SUV, she went with a second, equally honest answer. "I'm not going to be here for much longer, which would make any sort of hookup, for entertaining sex or otherwise, casual by definition. No offense, but when the call comes, I'm out of here."

The Denver P.D. was piloting an accelerated SWAT/ critical response training program that would leapfrog a few select forensic analysts straight into existing hazardous response teams—HRTs—where they would act as both technical support and boots on the ground. Although the TV shows made it seem like every CSI was a badge-wearing, gun-carrying cop, that was far from the case in most jurisdictions, where the cops were cops and the lab rats were...well, lab rats.

Going from the lab straight to hazardous response was a heck of a leap, but the members of Gigi's family were anything but conventional when it came to their ambitions. Whatever the Lynds did, they did it full throttle.

Alyssa glanced away. "I know you've only been here a few months, and we're just really getting to know each other. And it's not like I don't have other friends. Good friends. But...I like how you bring a new perspective to things around here. I wish—selfishly, I admit—that I had the budget to hire you away from Denver and keep you here in the lab. Thanks to Mayor Tightwad, I don't, so I have to think outside the box. If that means hunting down a few eligible bachelors..."

"Aw." Throat tightening, Gigi nudged the other woman gently with an elbow. "Thanks. But let's be realistic—I'm focusing on my career, which means you can't tempt me with a guy." The members of her family paired off in their mid-thirties, once they had a degree or two and a tenure track. She might not have inherited the Lynds' love of academia, but she had gotten their ambition in spades. "Besides it's not like I'm going to Mars or Timbuktu or something. I'll visit."

Alyssa shot her an "it won't be the same" look. "Are you sure—" Her phone rang with the plain digital ringtone that said it was official business. Immediately straightening away from Gigi's SUV, Alyssa pulled the phone and answered with a clipped, professional "McDermott, Forensics." But then her face softened. "Hello, McDermott, Homicide. What's up?"

Gigi started to wander off and give Alyssa privacy to talk to her husband. Baby McDermott's arrival was so imminent that most of the couple's business conversations inevitably turned personal, which made Gigi… Well, better to give them privacy.

"Station Fourteen?" Alyssa said, voice going worried. "Matt's station?"

The name stopped Gigi in her tracks.

Matt. As in Matt Blackthorn, head ranger of the state park's most remote outpost. The one guy she *had* noticed in Bear Claw, and not necessarily in a good way.

Her first impression had been positive—how could it not be? Blackthorn looked like one of the guys on the glossy brochures put out by the tourism bureau—edgy and gorgeous, with subtle bronzing and hard, commanding features that fit with his rumored Cherokee heritage. But unlike the professional models in the brochures, Blackthorn carried a rugged, purposeful energy and seemed to bring the mountain air down to the city with him—not the tame air of the ski slopes, but that of the wilderness, uncivilized and predatory.

The first moment she'd laid eyes on the big ranger, she had actually caught her breath.

They'd both been in the hallway outside of Tucker's office, her coming in, Blackthorn going out. And for a moment, something had sparked between them. At first, she had thought it was mutual attraction—the heated flash in the depths of his dark green eyes had resonated with the "hell, yeah" her hormones had been chorusing.

Then his gaze had shifted as he took in the rest of her, and his expression had tightened, killing the light of interest. Zap. Gone.

She didn't know what he had or hadn't seen in her, or what it had meant to him. She only knew that he'd touched the brim of the black felt hat he wore over his dark hair, and kept going. And the next time they'd crossed paths, when she'd done a briefing on a rash of parking-lot break-ins at several trailheads leading to the backcountry, Blackthorn had cut the conversation short enough to earn them a couple of raised eyebrows from the other cops and rangers involved in the meeting.

After that, she had avoided him. Not because he made her uncomfortable—she didn't give anyone that power—but because it didn't matter whether or not the head ranger of Station Fourteen liked her. She was there to work evidence for the Bear Claw City P.D. and prove to her bosses back home that she could fit herself seamlessly into an existing team like the BCCPD's crime lab. Blackthorn wasn't part of that world.

Unless there was a crime scene up at Station Fourteen. Then he was very much a part of her world—at least for the duration of the case.

Alyssa frowned. "Cassie's going to be tied up for the next few hours and there's no way I'm driving up to the middle of nowhere, never mind hiking to the site. Gigi can—" She broke off and glanced in Gigi's direction. "Okay. I can switch some stuff around and send Cassie, I guess. Tell him she'll be coming in behind the officers, and will need really good directions or a lead-in. We're shorthanded as it is. It won't do us any good to lose an analyst to the Forgotten."

Gigi barely heard the last part. She was too busy seething at the realization that Blackthorn had told Tucker—a former member of the Denver P.D. who had a direct pipeline to her bosses—that he didn't want her on the case.

"That backstabbing—" She bit off the snarl as Alyssa clicked her phone shut and regarded her curiously.

"What on earth is the problem between you and Matt?"

Taking a deep breath, Gigi slapped a layer of professionalism over her other emotions. "As far as I'm concerned, there's no problem. We met a couple of times, I was pleasant, he wasn't. End of story." At least it had been. Now she wanted a piece of him for trying to torpedo her. What had she ever done to him?

Nothing, that was what. Judgmental idiot.

"There's got to be more to it than that," Alyssa said. "It's not like him to be a jerk to anyone, especially a woman, never mind leaning on Tucker for something like this."

Gigi said through her teeth, "I've barely spoken to the man. If he took one look at me and decided he didn't like what he saw, that's his problem."

Alyssa's look went speculative, but she said only, "He told Tucker he didn't think you could handle the backcountry, that he'd rather wait for someone he didn't have to babysit."

"He…" Gigi counted to ten and reminded herself that it didn't matter what Blackthorn thought of her. Tucker was a fair guy and a top-notch cop, which meant he cared about results. "Fine, let's give Ranger Surly what he wants. I'll take over for Cassie and she can deal with his parking lot smash-and-grab."

But Alyssa shook her head, expression clouding. "It's way more than that. A few hours ago, two men attacked and injured one of his rangers—a woman named Tanya Dawes. They just airlifted her out."

"Oh." *Oh, damn.* Gigi exhaled in a rush, knowing full well that aggravated assault trumped any personal issues that might or might not exist between her and Blackthorn. "Is she going to be okay?"

"It looks like she took a serious blow to the head and may have some internal injuries. I guess she came around just long enough to tell Matt that two men had ambushed her."

"Sexual assault?"

"No sign of it, which is good. But the head injury… that's not good."

"Did she give Blackthorn any sort of description?"

"Nothing."

"Damn." Which meant that the crime scene analysis could be critical. "How do you want to handle it?"

Alyssa thought for a few seconds, then said, "I want you to head out to Station Fourteen. According to Matt, the scene took a beating when they airlifted her out, which makes you the better choice. Cassie is hell on wheels with the tech stuff, but you've got more experience with contaminated scenes. And if the problem between you and Matt is strictly an oil-and-water sort of thing, you'll deal with it. Right?"

Gigi nodded, already mentally reviewing the field kit she had with her, looking for gaps. "Of course. I've taken static on crime scenes before. I can handle myself."

More importantly, this wasn't about her and it sure wasn't about Blackthorn. She was there to do a job and she didn't intend to let anyone get in her way…especially not a park ranger with a great body and a nasty judgmental streak.

WHEN THE FIRST BCCPD vehicle churned into view in a cloud of dust, Matt was surprised to see Jack Williams at the wheel.

Williams, who topped six feet and had early salt in his chestnut hair though he was just on the downside of thirty, was one of the top detectives in Homicide. Born and raised in Bear Claw, Jack was the latest in a long line of Williamses to serve the BCCPD, and Matt's gut had long ago put the guy in the "solid cop" category.

As Williams climbed from the SUV, Matt headed over, hands in his pockets, still wearing his shotgun and knapsack over his shoulder. "I'll have to thank Tucker," he said to Williams. "This isn't exactly a case for Homicide, but I'm damn glad to see you."

The detective gave him a nod. "We take care of our own."

Matt didn't think he was talking about the close connection that had evolved between the P.D. and park service in Bear Claw, but didn't want to go down that road, so he said simply, "Thanks." He glanced over as a second cop got out of the SUV—a younger uniformed officer with a startling shock of white-blond hair and pale eyes that together made him look washed out beneath the late-summer sun. "New partner?"

"Billy Doran," Williams said by way of introduction. "Thanks to Mayor Cheapskate's latest round of cuts, we're down to under a dozen detectives trying to cover the whole damn city. Rather than partnering detectives, Tucker's got some of us teaming up with uniforms."

Despite his one-time interest in politics, Matt had stayed well clear of Bear Claw's issues, just as he largely avoided the city itself. He hadn't moved to Station Fourteen to get involved in city stuff, after all. Even so, he knew that Mayor Percy Proudfoot had been taking some serious hacks at the budget in an effort to turn around a huge budget deficit. The P.D. in particular was having to get creative.

He sent the kid a nod. "Doran." Turning back to Williams, he said, "I'll lead you guys in, then come back down for Cassie when she gets here." He hesitated. "There's something I didn't get a chance to tell Tucker." He told them about the feather, patted his buttoned pocket. "You guys want it?"

"Keep it until Cass gets here," Williams said. "It's probably better not to move it around more than necessary. But don't be surprised if she wants your shirt, too, in case there's transfer." He grinned. "Just watch what you say if she does. Last guy who made a sexist joke about the crime scene girls got the rough side of Alyssa's tongue, and then spent some quality time directing traffic for a sewer repair crew, courtesy of Chief Mendoza."

"I'll keep that in mind." Actually, it didn't matter to him whether the Bear Claw analysts were women or Martians, as long as they got the job done.

"Grab the gear," Williams said to Doran. To Matt, he said, "Lead on and let's see what these bastards left us."

"Not much that I could see. The scene is pretty torn up."

Sure enough, once he got them up there, Williams shook his head. "You weren't kidding. What isn't bare rock is a frigging mess." He sent Doran to take pictures and notes, but didn't look optimistic. "I have a feeling our best bet is going to be talking to Tanya when she wakes up."

Matt nodded, partly in thanks for the word choice. *When* she woke up. Not if. When.

The detective said, "Want to run me through what you saw? Maybe being up here will kick loose something new."

"Of course." Matt started right from the moment he heard Cochran's first shout, but it was becoming rote. And, really, he hadn't been there when it counted.

By the time Doran was done, Williams was ready to head back down to the station and question the Cochrans, so Matt led them back to the vehicles.

On the way, he radioed Bert for an update and got confirmation that Tanya's injuries were from an attack rather than a fall, along with the grim news that she was still unconscious and the early scan results weren't good. *Damn it.*

Forcing his emotions down where they belonged, Matt asked, "How about the CSI? Did she come through the station yet?" If Tanya wasn't waking up, they needed to get moving on the scene. Every minute they wasted was another minute the perps were using to get away… or plan another attack.

"Yeah. She should be there any minute."

Sure enough, the cops were loading up their SUV when the radio on his hip squalled a broken transmission. All he caught was a woman's voice and the words "almost there."

The dust kicked up by Williams's departing SUV was just clearing when a new cloud took shape and a nearly identical vehicle appeared coming the other way.

Matt checked his watch and was surprised to see that even though it felt like days had passed, it had only been five or six hours of real time. That meant they had a couple of hours of daylight left.

They would need it, too. It wouldn't be easy to truck in lights, and there wasn't much chance of an airdrop. Tucker had already given him the heads up that the P.D. was getting pressure from higher up the food chain— aka Mayor Proudfoot's office—to keep Tanya's assault on the down low and not over-commit resources.

The official line was that the attack wasn't all that different from an in-city mugging, and while Tanya would get some preference as a ranger, the P.D. shouldn't go overboard. The real rationale, though, was even simpler: Bear Claw City was hurting for money and couldn't afford to lose any tourists.

Matt hated the equation, the politics.

The SUV cruised in going too fast and kicked up

dust, suggesting that Cassie, too, knew they were racing the sun. Grit hazed things as the door swung open and she got out, hauling a heavy-looking tackle box with her.

He headed over, extending a hand. "Let me grab that for…" He trailed off, stopping dead as his gut fisted on a surge of heat mixed with dismay.

The woman coming toward him wasn't the business-like blonde he'd been expecting.

Not even close.

A sizzle shot through him at the sight of a sharp, tri-angular face beneath a crooked cap of shiny dark hair. He told himself the sensation was dismay, because he sure as hell shouldn't be feeling anything else toward a woman like Gigi Lynd.

Gigi. It sounded like it should come with a French label and an import tariff. And from her trendy haircut and unbalanced ear piercings—one on the right, three on the left—to the silver-gilded tips of her gleaming lizard-skin boots—black today rather than the purple she had been wearing before, but equally as impracti-cal—she didn't belong anywhere near the backcountry. Or him.

His pulse raced. He was going to kill Tucker.

Her white button-down was open just low enough to show a hint of cleavage, and the black belt that rode below her narrow waist had a gleam of silver that drew the eye.

"No," he said without preamble as she squared off opposite him. "I want one of the others."

Her smoky gray eyes narrowed. "You made that clear when you trashed me to McDermott."

"I didn't—" He broke off, guilt stinging because he hadn't exactly trashed her, but he'd made it clear he didn't think she had the backcountry experience or analytical chops to handle the case. "Look, it's nothing personal."

"Bull. You took one look at me and decided that I was incompetent based on, what? Some eyeliner and a little bling?" She flicked the more heavily pierced of her earlobes. "Fine, whatever, that's your problem not mine. But you're one-hundred percent right that this *shouldn't* be personal. You don't have to like me. Just get out of my way and let me do my job."

The guilt twisted harder because she was right. He'd snap judged her, hard, which was so far from his usual style it was practically alien.

That didn't mean she was the right analyst for the job, though.

He glanced up the trail. "Look, I'm sorry about the attitude. It's just… Believe it or not, I don't doubt your competence—McDermott wouldn't have leaned on his contacts in Denver to get you if you weren't the best crime scene analyst available. But you're a long way from home, and the backcountry isn't anything like the city. Alyssa, Cassie and Maya have all worked scenes out here before. You haven't."

She pierced him with a cool look. "Yet they sent me, even after you told Tucker not to. Want to take a guess as to why?"

"I don't want to… Damn it." He jammed both hands in his pockets, knowing he was beaten. And what was more, he was dead wrong. She hadn't done a damn thing to deserve his suspicion. It wasn't her fault that she was the first woman in a long time to make him want to stop and take a second, longer look. Maybe a taste.

And that so wasn't happening.

He didn't know what she saw in his face, but her expression softened. "I'm sorry about what happened to Tanya. And under the circumstances, I'm even sorry that my being here bothers you. But back in Denver I was the analyst of choice for badly contaminated scenes. Right before I left, I worked a murder scene at the edge of an eroded riverbank the day after a downpour. And yes, we got the guy." She paused. "You want to get the two men who hurt your ranger? Then take me to your scene… and make it fast, because we're burning daylight."

Matt wasn't sure which was worse: having been so thoroughly set down…or knowing that he was going to have to stick right with her. Because he'd be damned if anyone else got hurt on his watch.

"Okay," he said. "Okay, yeah." Mind already skimming ahead to what he was going to need out of the Jeep, he whipped off his shirt and held it out. "You're going to want this."

It wasn't until she gave a strangled gasp, eyes going wide, that he realized he was standing there bare-chested, and she had no clue why he'd just stripped down.

Heat washed through him. Oh, hell. That was so not cool.

"There's evidence in the front pocket," he said quickly. "A feather Tanya was holding when I got to her. Williams said you would want the shirt, too, for transfer." He started to apologize, would have except for one thing:

She was staring at his chest.

He stilled, watching a faint flush climb her throat and work its way to her face as she swallowed. Then she jerked her eyes to his, and the blush hit hard.

Electricity raced over his skin, tightening his body as they stared at each other for a three count.

She recovered first, with a gulp and a small shiver that he felt deep in his gut. "Um," she said, voice huskier than it had been a moment earlier, "hold that thought."

When she put down the tackle box that contained her field kit, he thought…hell, he didn't know what he thought. His brain was gone, melted by whatever had just telegraphed between them. So when she rummaged and came up with a large evidence bag, he just stared at it for a second.

Then reality returned and his brain reassembled itself.

Tanya. Evidence. The crime scene.

What the hell was he doing?

Without a word, he folded the shirt and tucked it into the bag, watched her seal it and scrawl her name on the first line of the evidence chain. Then he turned away and headed for his Jeep, saying over his shoulder, "Let me grab my jacket and we can hit the trail."

And as he led her up to Candle Rock, he worked like hell to get his head screwed back on straight. Because he couldn't afford to let himself get distracted in a crisis situation. Bad things happened when he did.

Chapter Three

Wow. That was all Gigi's brain could formulate as she followed Blackthorn along a narrow game trail that led up a sharply rocky incline.

Wow, he had a seriously fine body beneath that drab, tan-and-green park service uniform. His sleek bronze skin covered sculpted muscles, its perfection marred by two scars, one high on his shoulder, the other wrapping around his waistline.

Wow, that had been the hottest stand-and-stare moment of her life. Her blood was still humming, her coordination slightly off as her body focused inward.

And wow, this was way outside her comfort zone.

It had been a while since she had made the time or effort, but she'd had her share of relationships, all based on affection, attraction, and the freedom to move on when the time came.

Those relationships had been fun. Satisfying. And not once, not even in the bedroom, had any of those guys lit her up the way she had just ignited from nothing more than seeing Blackthorn's chest.

Even now, as she scanned the rocks and scrub for

scuff marks, the image of his naked torso seemed burned onto her retinas.

Temporary insanity. That was all it was. They'd both had their tempers up, and his adrenaline had probably been pumping for hours. More, she had been disarmed by the way he had backed down, owning his bad behavior when she called him on it.

In her experience, that wasn't the way real jerks operated. Which meant…well, it didn't matter what it meant. Her gut said he was complicated, and she didn't have any room in her life for personal complications. She was there to do her job…which was about evidence, not ogling.

Deliberately, she forced her mind back on track.

The bagged shirt was tucked in the bottom of her field kit. She would process the feather back in the lab, where she could keep absolute track of the environment. But she already knew some of the assessments she would need to make: Was it real or fake? Where had it come from? Why had Tanya been clutching it?

The last question wasn't really part of an analyst's job—it was up to the cops and attorneys to turn the data into a story.

But then again, she lived outside the box.

When Blackthorn hit the top of the high ridge, he paused and turned back to her. Surprise flickered when he saw that she was only a few paces behind him and not even breathing particularly hard.

She grinned. "When I was in my early teens, my parents went on a survivalist kick and decided all four of us kids needed to know how to take care of ourselves, no matter what. Our family vacations turned into something out of *Survivor* for a few years. Yosemite, the Sonoran Desert, Alaska… Some of it seemed like torture at the time, but looking back, it wasn't. It's just the way my family operates."

"As survivalists?"

"As the best at whatever we choose to do. Usually it's academics. In my case, crime scene analysis."

He held her eyes for a moment, then nodded slowly. "Point taken."

"Then let's get to work." She gestured around them. "How are you at tracking?"

"Fair to good, but when we came up this way the first time, I was looking more for four-legged predators than two-legged tracks. I can't swear to it, but I don't think there were any fresh footprints other than Cochran's at that point, and even those were pretty faint. I took a closer look around once Tanya had been airlifted out, but nothing jumped out at me." He grimaced. "Frankly, given the rock, hardpan and loose gravel, we're not looking good for tracks."

"Hopefully I'll have better luck."

"It's a mess down there."

"So I heard." But as she moved up beside him at the crest of the ridge, she sucked in a breath. "Okay. Yeah. That's a mess."

Their vantage point overlooked an oblong flattened bowl that fell away into a dry riverbed on one side. There was a brushed-clean spot where the helicopter had come and gone; ropes snaking across the shale, which was gouged where they had been moved and dragged; and a scattering of detritus in the bottom of the wash.

Although she gave Blackthorn points for not cleaning

up the med techs' leftovers after Tanya was airlifted, the overall effect was not encouraging.

He shot her a look from beneath lowered brows. "Tell me you can do something with it."

"I've seen entire cases hinge on a few strands of hair or a fingernail scraping," she said. Which wasn't quite an answer, so she added, "I've worked under worse conditions. At least here I won't have to waste time going through a ton of alley garbage that has zero relevance to the case."

"Small blessings."

"In this job, you take what you can get." *And you'd better watch it, we seem to be having a semi-normal conversation,* she thought but didn't say. Instead, she nodded to the shotgun he carried slung over his shoulder. "I'm going to be pretty involved for the next couple of hours. You'll keep lookout?"

Something shifted in the dark green depths of his eyes, and he nodded. "Nobody else is getting hurt on my watch."

Sensing he didn't want to hear that he wasn't responsible for what had happened to Tanya, she gripped his forearm briefly. "Thanks."

As she moved past him, she felt his surprise just as clearly as she had felt his leashed strength through the thin layer of his windbreaker. She wasn't sure if his shock had come from the touch or the fact that they were getting along, but she would take it.

She had a feeling she would be better to have him a little off balance around her, not vice versa.

When she was halfway down the incline, he called, "Hey. Gigi."

He gave it the softer pronunciation, as though they were in Paris rather than the middle of nowhere.

She turned back and found him backlit by the afternoon sun, a solitary figure on the ridgeline. She had to clear her throat before she said, "Yeah?"

"I'm sorry I was a jerk to you back in the city. You're okay."

"Be still my heart." But she grinned when she said it. "And my name is Gigi," she corrected, giving it the harder sound. "It's short for Greta Grace, so you don't need to get fancy with it. Or with me."

He didn't say anything, just gave her a slow nod, but she felt his eyes follow her the rest of the way down.

Then she tuned him out and got to work.

The next ninety minutes were a focused blur of photographs, sample bags and jars, and a whole lot of frustration at the lack of what she thought of as "big foam finger evidence"—the kind that pointed straight to an answer, or at least a new set of questions.

Granted, that was the exception rather than the norm, but still, she had been hoping for a quick break in the case.

By the time the sun dipped behind the mountains and the sky went pink around the edges, she was finishing up her preliminary round of collection. She locked her kit, and hauled its now considerable weight back up the ridgeline, where Blackthorn stood guard, silhouetted against the dusk.

He gave her a long, unreadable look. "All set?"

"With the first step, anyway. Now it's time for me to put in some serious lab hours."

He took the case from her without asking, his fingers brushing against hers. "But you're not hopeful."

"I'm always hopeful," she corrected, telling herself it was impossible to get a whole-body tingle from that small contact. "But in this case, I'm not very optimistic. I didn't see anything I could link straight to Tanya's attackers. Between that and the beating her radio took, it was like she was dropped..." She trailed off, sudden excitement sparking. "Wait a second. Let me see your radio."

He unclipped it from his belt and handed it over. "Bert can hook you up if you need a patch-through back to the lab or something."

"That won't be necessary."

She took the sturdy unit, which, aside from being bright yellow rather than matte black, was very like the ones used by the HRTs back home, with long-range capabilities, GPS, a digital display...and a hinged faceplate that usually broke off within the first few weeks of use. It was the one design flaw in an otherwise solid piece of equipment.

Blackthorn's still had its faceplate in place, though, and had a couple of upgrades she hadn't seen before. "Is this new?" she asked.

"They arrived last week."

Damn it, she had assumed Tanya's faceplate was long gone—and because she had made an assumption, she almost missed the evidence...or lack thereof. "Do all of your rangers carry the same model?"

"Yeah, they're interchangeable. We just grab one off the charger in my office. Why?"

She looked up at him, pulse kicking. "Did hers still have its faceplate when she left this morning?"

He thought for a second, then nodded. "Yeah, I'm sure it did." He looked back down to the scene, making the connection. "It could've bounced pretty far. Even given that some of her injuries came from an attack, she still hit hard when she fell."

"Or we were meant to think she did."

He went very still, eyes darkening as he slowly looked down, then back at her. "Damn. I saw it."

"The faceplate?"

He shook his head. "No, that there was a problem with the way she and the radio had fallen." His expression went distant as he replayed the scene in his head. "She was lying flat on her back, kind of sprawled, with the radio a few feet away. There weren't any impact marks…but there was a smoothed-flat place." He refocused, met her eyes. "Like someone had been there, swept his tracks, and then tossed the radio down after the fact."

"All we're going to have on that is your statement," she cautioned, "and my not finding the faceplate doesn't necessarily mean it wasn't there. I can't use a negative to prove a positive." But they were onto something. She was sure of it. "We're going to need more."

His expression firmed. "Then we'll find it." He paused. "You think this is a secondary scene. A dump site."

She nodded. "That's how it reads to me. And it's consistent with her Jeep not being right in this area." The vehicle's GPS wasn't registering and it hadn't been sighted along what should have been Tanya's morning route, either.

"So we have another crime scene to find."

With another man she might've told him to stay out of the way and let the cops do their job. Given that he was the local expert, though, and the P.D. was spread very thin, she said, "The faceplate is going to be a needle in a really large haystack, and there's no telling whether the Jeep is even still in the park. Take your pick."

A muscle ticked at the corner of his jaw. "The Jeep would be an easier target, obviously, but an air search is going to be difficult to pull off, if not impossible. All the working birds are tied up fighting the wildfires, and a bunch are down for repairs. We've put out feelers to other parks, other options, but so far we haven't come up with much." His head came up and his shoulders squared. "So we go old school."

"A foot search?" She looked around, unable to imagine any search being able to cover the vast, varied terrain that made up the state park.

"Yeah. I'll line up off-duty rangers, any of the on-duty rangers who can be spared, maybe even some expert hikers." He gestured down the ridge toward their vehicles. They went down together, side by side. "I'll get the search organized for first light tomorrow. We'll start with her sector and work out from there." He shot her a look. "You want in?"

"Absolutely." The invitation kicked a warm buzz through her, not just because he was admitting she could handle the backcountry, but because it felt good to be planning something rather than just gathering data. That was a big part of why she wanted to make the jump from lab rat to HRT—she wanted to do both.

Within minutes, Blackthorn was on the radio with three other station heads, getting their cooperation and coordinating the mobilization.

As they neared the parking area, she shot him a side-long look, struck by the change in him. His face was animated, his green eyes fierce and intense. More, his voice now carried a heavy weight of command that had the heads of the other stations practically snapping to attention.

She remembered the scars on his shoulder and waist, belatedly recognizing them as bullet strikes. *Ex-military,* she thought, and pegged him as an officer. But if he had that kind of background, why had he buried himself out in the middle of nowhere?

New interest stirred, not just for the sexy package, but for the man inside it. *He's complicated,* she reminded herself. But this time she found herself thinking that maybe she could handle some complications for the few more weeks she would be in Bear Claw.

Especially if those complications looked—and sounded—like Ranger Blackthorn in get-it-done mode.

"Thanks, Harvey. I'll be in touch," he said into the radio, then clicked it off and returned it to his belt. They had reached their vehicles, which were dark shapes in the gathering dusk. His shadow merged with that of his Jeep, and his voice seemed to come from the darkness when he said, "The cops collected the hikers' clothes and stuff, said they would log it all into evidence for you. And Williams suggested you take a look around the station house, particularly Tanya's room."

"I've done some work in profiling and victimology, and have helped Jack out on a couple of cases. He's hoping I'll see something that could point toward a motive."

"You don't think this was random?" His voice carried a new edge. "What aren't you telling me?"

Suddenly reminded that he wasn't technically part of the investigation, she said, "There's nothing to tell yet. We're still exploring options."

He moved in closer and dropped his voice an octave. "Hiding behind the official line, Gigi?"

Nerves stirred low in her belly, coiling her tight, but she met his eyes and said levelly, "I'm just trying to do my job, Blackthorn, so don't crowd me. And don't make the mistake of thinking you're something you're not." He wasn't a cop, couldn't expect her to keep him fully in the loop unless he cleared it with the higher-ups.

He growled something under his breath, but eased back a step. He tried the door of her SUV, found it locked, and set her field kit on the ground. "You'll want to follow me back to the station. Wouldn't want you getting lost."

He headed for his Jeep with long-legged strides, unslinging his shotgun and knapsack as he went.

Gigi watched him go, trying not to be fascinated. He held himself apart but felt responsible, knew how to lead but had buried himself far from any troops, respected competence but wanted to be calling the shots…and was attracted and didn't want to be.

No, she had definitely been right the first time around.

She didn't have the mental energy to deal with him right now, not even for some short-term fun.

Too bad, she thought, remembering the gleam of bronze skin, the pucker of two bullet scars, one high, one low. Then she shook her head, climbed into her ride, and focused on the puzzle of two attackers, one missing faceplate…and a gut feeling that said there was far more to this case than anyone suspected.

Chapter Four

Matt kept it under warp speed as he led the way to the station house, but he was tempted to hit the gas and see if he could outrun his anger and frustration.

The case and the woman had him badly off-kilter, leaving him raw and reactive…and those were two things that didn't belong anywhere near an investigation like this one. If he didn't pull it together, he wasn't going to be any use to his rangers, the cops, or Gigi. And the fact that his mind slotted her into a category of her own just proved that he was badly out of whack. He didn't prioritize like that. Ever.

The radio crackled. "Hey, boss, you out there?"

"Yeah, Bert. What's up?"

"We're up to five stations sending rangers for the search, and three others are pending. We're going to be ready to roll at first light."

"Good." He would run it past Tucker, but couldn't imagine there would be a problem. The searchers all had training, and it wouldn't cost the city a dime. "How's Tanya?"

"No change."

"Damn." The station lights came into view, piercing the darkness up ahead. "We're here."

He parked the Jeep in its usual spot, while Gigi unknowingly took Tanya's.

She locked her field kit in a strongbox in the back of her SUV, pocketed the key and turned for the station. She hesitated when she saw him standing there, watching her, then met his stare, unspeaking, as if to say, "Here I am. What are you going to do about it?"

That was the question, wasn't it?

As before, heat laced the air between them. This time, though, there was a softer layer, one that came from the realization that she was smart and dedicated, and was busting her ass to help find Tanya's attackers.

He wasn't looking to get involved, hadn't been for a long time, but there she was.

And he was in serious trouble.

"Bert!" he shouted, louder and sharper than he'd intended.

Boots thudded and the older ranger appeared in the screened doorway of the faux log cabin. "Boss?"

"I need you to show Ms. Lynd around the station for me."

He needed some space, and he needed it now.

GIGI WATCHED HIM GO, trying to suppress a twinge of what should have been irritation but felt more like hurt. She had thought they had called a truce of sorts out at the scene. Apparently not.

"Please excuse Matt," Bert said blandly. "He was raised by a grizzly."

She glanced over at the older ranger, who had silver-shot hair and laugh lines at the corners of his weathered eyes. "Not wolves?"

He shook his head. "Nope, too social. We're pretty sure it was a single bachelor grizzly of the pissed-off variety—the kind that snarls when cornered." He toed open the screen door and held it for her. "Come on up. I'll show you Tanya's room and whatever else you want to see. Anything that'll help."

"Thanks." Forcing her mind off Blackthorn's Dr. Jekyll and Ranger Surly routine, she followed Bert into the station.

The building was T-shaped, with the main entrance— the public area—centered on the crossbars.

They entered a long, narrow room that was divided roughly in half by a waist-high counter, with bathrooms on either side: men on the left, women on the right. A door centered on the back wall led to the longer bunkhouse wing that finished the T-shape.

The walls of the front room were lined with maps, brochures and copies of the fliers the park service put out each year, complete with instructions on bear avoidance, trail safety and what to do in the event of an emergency. On the other side of the counter—the rangers' side—the papers hung on the walls and office cubbies leaned more toward emergency numbers and scrawled notes.

Bert waved her through a flip-up pass in the counter, then gestured to a small desk. "That's Tanya's. So are the pictures."

A row of sketches were tacked along the wall to the right of the desk. Tanya had captured dozens of moments: a stark, barren landscape of rocks and stunted trees; a doe and fawn silhouetted atop a sparsely forested ridgeline; ghostly wisps of mist rising off the surface of a pond as a coyote paused to drink; the curl of a fern, so mundane until seen through eyes that found something beautiful in it; a hawk's flight, sketched so sparsely as to be mere suggestions of line and motion, except for the creature's head and its bright, fierce eyes.

But Gigi's attention was immediately drawn to a deft caricature off to one side. In it, a handsome young man—presumably Jim Feeney—and Bert were horsing around together there in the station. There was a hint of a Stetson-shadow just visible through a doorway, putting Blackthorn in the picture. Sort of.

"She's talented," Gigi commented past the sudden tightening of her throat.

Bert reached out to brush his thumb across the bold *T* at the bottom of the caricature. "She hasn't woken up yet."

There was guilt beneath the pain, just like with Matt. It made Gigi think that maybe rangers weren't as different from cops as she had thought—both protected their people and their territories, and took it very seriously when one of their own went down in the line.

"Tell me about her," she said.

"She's a good kid, a good ranger, and practically has eyes in the back of her head. Whoever these guys are, they would've had to know the backcountry to get the drop on her."

Which narrowed things down, but not by much. "Does she have any enemies you know about? Anyone who would want to hurt her?" Williams would have asked the standard questions, but it didn't hurt to repeat them.

He shook his head. "No way. She wasn't that kind of person."

"How about a boyfriend?"

"She and Jim flirted, but I don't think it was serious, at least not on her part. And before you ask, no, he wasn't mad about it, and yes, he was here all morning. He's at the hospital right now, driving himself nuts—just like we all are—wondering if there was something he could've done to prevent this and hoping to hell she wakes up soon." His voice had sharpened, but before she could say something to bring things down a notch, his shoulders slumped. "Sorry. This really sucks."

"Yeah. It does." She touched his arm in sympathy. "I'm sorry to make you go through it again."

"Don't be. I'll do whatever I can to help. It's just…" He paused, then said slowly, "The rangers who work the outer stations tend to be out here for a reason. Some because they need space, others because they plain don't like being around other people. Tanya is one of the first kind, or at least she was when she got here. Lately, though, she's gone from this—" he tapped one of the lonely, barren landscapes "—to this—" his finger moved to the doe and her fawn "—to this." He touched the caricature.

"She was healing from something?" Maybe something that had made enemies?

"That'd be my take. She didn't talk about it, though, at least not with me. Just said she had made mistakes and wanted to move on. Recently, though, she seemed to be coming out of her shell."

"Because of her relationship with Jim?" Or was there something else going on?

"Maybe. Or maybe it was just time. Who knows?" He straightened away from the pictures. "Come on. I'll show you her room."

Gigi followed him through to the bunkhouse wing, where a wide hallway was flanked on either side by rows of closed doors. The hall ended in a set of double doors leading out, their windows showing the pitch black of night beyond.

"That's the boss's office," Bert said, jerking a thumb at the first on the left. "The rest are all dorm-type rooms from back when this was a research station. Matt's house was the old observatory. He converted it when he came out here five, six years ago."

"You don't seem like the kind of guy who has trouble being around people."

He shot her a look that said he knew exactly what she was asking. "My wife and I separated a couple of years ago, which made the 'getting away' part attractive. This is the perfect setup—close enough to the city that I can visit my one kid who stayed local for college and see the other two when they come back to town. Not to mention that room and board is included, which helps when you're scraping to pay three tuitions."

"And Jim?"

"Won't last out here much longer. He came for the hiking and stayed because he was enjoying himself—and maybe a bit to see how things would go with Tanya— but I doubt he'll be here come winter. He doesn't need it the way the rest of us do." A muted crackle of static had his head whipping around. "I need to get that." He pointed to the end of the hall. "Her room is the last door on your right. It's not locked."

She watched him disappear through the door to the main room, wishing she had asked about Blackthorn just then. He had been there six years, and…what? Stalled? Healed? Found exactly what he was looking for?

As she headed for Tanya's room, a faint shiver touched her nape. Under other circumstances, she would have thought it was her instincts telling her to watch her back, but she was safe in the station, and she knew darn well the threat wasn't coming from outside.

She was on the borderline of a major crush.

And she needed to stop it.

"Okay. I'm stopping." Blanking her mind of the lingering images of Blackthorn standing guard, silhouetted against the setting sun, she took a deep breath and pushed through into Tanya's room.

Since it wasn't a crime scene, she didn't need to print the doorknob or wear protective gear. She just closed the door behind her, flipped the light switch, and stood there for a moment.

The room was maybe twice the width of the twin-size bed that sat along one wall beneath a colorful quilt. A desk and short chest of drawers took up the other wall, leaving only a narrow runway down the center of the space. The door was centered on one end, a window on the other.

The small space might have resembled a cell if it weren't for the warm colors and bold textures decorating it, and the profusion of sketches tacked to the walls.

The pictures were similar to the ones out in the main station—mostly nature scenes, with a few caricatures of the other rangers, done on newer paper and layered atop the others. There was also a detailed sketch of blond, good-looking Jim, posed casually and looking at the artist with a seriously devilish glint that practically screamed "let's get out of here and have some fun."

Heart tugging for the victim, Gigi took another, longer look around the room, trying to get a sense of Tanya—or, more importantly, what she had been trying to escape.

Most everything in the room seemed to belong to her present incarnation: hiking and climbing equipment, sturdy clothes, trail maps, a few field guides on local plants and animals, a couple of paperbacks and a cache of chocolate bars. There was winter gear under the bed… and behind it, a set of high-end downhill skis, boots and other equipment, carefully wrapped in worn-looking plastic, as if they had been stored away for longer than just the summer. Gigi filed the observation and moved on.

There was a laptop on the small bureau, but it was wearing a layer of folded laundry, suggesting it wasn't used all that often. Making a mental note to see if Jack wanted her to bring it down to the P.D. for the techies to look at, she took a quick rifle through Tanya's bathroom stuff and then flipped through the books.

A folded piece of paper fluttered from one of the field guides, slipping from between a couple of pages at the back before she could catch it, or see what it had marked.

It proved to be another sketch: a quick pencil study of a dark-haired man in his mid-twenties, long-nosed and serious-eyed, sitting on an oblong boulder that jutted out across the impressive backdrop of a huge waterfall. The paper was soft with age and worn along the fold line, and the man looked oddly familiar, though she couldn't immediately place him.

Did he look like someone a girl would disappear into the backcountry to forget?

Instincts humming, she secured the picture in one of the evidence bags she had brought with her, and tucked it into an inner pocket of her windbreaker. She thought about bagging the field guide, but decided to come back for it later if the picture turned out to be important. Tanya's things weren't going anywhere, and for all she knew, the guy was a family member, the waterfall far away.

That was the tricky part about victimology: it wasn't always clear how the puzzle fit together until long after the fact, if at all.

And there weren't any big-foam-finger clues here, at least not that she could tell at this point. Which meant it was time to head back down to the city and hit the lab.

Letting herself out of Tanya's room, she stepped into the hallway. She heard radio traffic from the main room, and raised her voice to call, "Hey Bert, can you—"

Movement flashed in her peripheral vision and a heavy blow slammed into her from behind, driving her to her knees. *Ambush!*

Panic flared at the sight of a man dressed in dark clothes standing over her, his face obscured by shadows.

Part of her recorded details—*six foot, shaved head, athletic*—while another had her shouting, "Help! They're in the station!"

Her body reacting more from training than thought,

she tucked and rolled, then lashed out with a foot. She connected and her attacker fell back with a curse. But before she could follow up, the lights went out, plunging the hallway into pitch darkness.

"Come on!" a voice called from farther down the hall. "Forget about the stuff. The fire'll take care of these two, along with everything else."

Fire? Heart hammering with new terror, Gigi screamed, "Bert? Help!"

It was a mistake; her attacker oriented and slammed her aside. She swung another kick, but didn't connect with anything, and moments later feet pounded away from her.

A door slammed, and then there were two dull thuds. Seconds later, she heard the crash of breaking glass on either side of her, behind several of the closed bunkroom doors, one of them Tanya's.

Then there was an ominous *whoomping* sound that had her instincts sparking with terror as she identified the sounds: the man had thrown Molotov cocktails into the dorm rooms!

Worse, she could see the orange glow through the exit-door windows, smell it on the thickening air.

Atavistic fear flared and she froze in place, blanking on everything except the insidious crackle and yellow-orange glow. Her brain jammed, and all she could think was: *impossible.* This wasn't happening, couldn't be happening.

Except it was.

"Help! Fire!" She screamed it so loud that her throat went instantly raw. The pain snapped her back to reality, adrenaline cleared her head, and the two together got her moving, fast.

She remembered seeing extinguishers, didn't know where they were, remembered seeing smoke alarms and sprinklers, didn't know why they weren't going off.

She lunged for the doors that led outside, but they didn't budge, not even when she twisted the deadbolt back and forth. They were jammed from the other side.

Forget about the stuff. The fire'll take care of these two, along with everything else.

Her stomach roiled. Oh, God. They were trapped, and she had missed something important. Something the men—there had to be more than two—would kill to protect.

The air was heavy with smoke, making her cough.

Her mind was jumbled with half-memorized crisis response protocols, terror, and the drive that made her one of the best at her job. She reeled back to Tanya's room and banged open the door, noticing too late that the knob burned her palm.

Flames roared greedily, leaping at her, and a wall of heat sent her staggering backward. Instead of providing an exit, the broken window fed oxygen to the flames that engulfed the bed and desk, curling the sketches to blackness and then racing toward her.

"No!" She reeled back and slammed the door. A rasping moan brought her whipping around. "Bert!"

With no light except for the unearthly glow of the fire that was spreading outside, along the building's too-dry exterior, she stumbled in the darkness, feeling her way to the door that led to the front room. The knob was warm but not scalding, so she pushed through, coughing when she tried to breathe the hot, smoke-laden air.

There were emergency lights on in the main room, but the fire outside was worse, licking past the level of the windows. She saw Bert sprawled in the corner near the men's room, but raced across the room and tried the front door first. It was locked.

Her pulse thudding so loudly it almost drowned out the fire's insidious crackle, she crouched over the older ranger, breathing the thinner air near the floor. He stirred and groaned, but wasn't fully conscious.

She checked his pulse; his skin was baking in the increasing burn of the air around them, but his heartbeat was sure and steady. "Bert? It's Gigi. It's going to be okay. You're going to be okay. I'm going to get us out of here." But how?

He stirred weakly, rolled onto his side, and started struggling to rise, but was clearly out of it, wobbly and incoherent, coughing wretchedly in the smoky air. She took off her windbreaker, draped it over his head and ordered, "Stay down."

She lurched to her feet and stumbled to the nearest window and wept when it didn't budge.

Heart hammering, fear jamming a hard lump in her throat, she felt along the counter, searching for a radio, an extinguisher, something—anything—that would help.

The air scorched her skin, and the roaring sound coming from behind her suggested that the bunkhouse was fully ablaze.

Her fingers brushed something fastened beneath the counter, and she nearly sobbed in relief when she recognized the butt of a shotgun, secured out of public sight but ready if needed. Her hands shook so badly that it took her several tries to yank it free, but she finally got it.

Staying low, she pumped it, took aim, and fired both barrels through the window.

The blasts deafened her, but she raced to the window, stuck her head through and screamed, "Blackthorn, help! *Fire!*"

Chapter Five

The gunshots and distant scream rang in Matt's ears like a nightmare. *Fire!*

He broke off in the middle of saying something to Tucker on the phone and spun toward the far window of the living room in his house, which was a short hike from the station.

His gut fisted at the sight of a sickly glow where the station's lights should have been.

In the split second it took him to process the shock, a dark figure streaked past in silhouette, brake lights flashed from a rolling vehicle he damn well hadn't heard pull up, and gravel spat as the culprits accelerated away. "Son of a *bitch!*"

"What's wrong?"

"Get whatever eyes you can on the access road and send men up here to Fourteen, a fire chopper if you can get one. Someone just lit the station and took off!"

Gigi's scream echoed in Matt's head as he jammed his radio on his belt and took off at a dead run.

As he skidded down the short path between his quarters and the station house, the ranger in him noted the wind strength and direction and hoped to hell the flames wouldn't jump to the nearby trees. The rest of him just saw a damned inferno where a T-shaped building should've been.

Flames shot up from the bunkhouse windows and roof, eating through the too-dry wood like it was fresh newspaper. The front wasn't yet fully consumed, but fiery fingers of yellow-orange twined along the logs and licked at the pitched roof.

For a second, Matt thought that he was too damn late. Then he caught movement at one of the windows and—*thank God*—heard Gigi call, "Blackthorn!"

He bolted for the spot just as a figure came through the broken window, movements slow and uncoordinated, body too big to be Gigi. Bert.

Matt surged forward to help, his mind locking on the awful knowledge that the bastards had lit his station and he hadn't been there to stop it.

"Grab him!" Gigi's voice was raspy, her eyes wet and afraid, but she was wholly focused on getting a woozy Bert out first. "Watch the glass. I had to shoot it out."

The window was shattered and jagged, the frame wedged shut by a narrow chunk of wood shoved into the top.

Murderous rage boiled through him, but he held himself in check as he helped Bert down, then tucked a shoulder under his arm to prop him up. "Come on," he said to her, holding out his free hand. "Jump down."

The air was barely breathable, the heat unbearable. It seared through his clothes and crisped his skin. Small cinders were starting to break loose and sail up into the sky.

Gigi slithered through the window in a practiced,

feet-first rush, but when she landed, staggered a few steps and went down on one knee, coughing.

He caught her by the arm and hauled her up, then started half-dragging, half-carrying both of them away from the blaze.

She leaned into him, gasping for air, trying to get out information between her ragged breaths. "White guy, maybe six foot, one-eighty…said something about 'the stuff'…evidence…" She stopped dead and yanked away with a gasp, eyes going wide in shock. "The *picture!*"

"Who—" He broke off when she whirled and ran back toward the station. Blood congealing, Matt bellowed, "Gigi, damn it, *no!*"

"I know who he is!" She vaulted back through the window.

"Gigi!"

"Go." Bert pulled away from him and stood swaying. "You go get her. I'll call it in."

"I already did." Matt yanked his radio off his belt and handed it over. "Tucker's probably still on the channel." Then he took off, running back into the fire after a crazy woman.

He was still a dozen paces away when something crashed inside, and flames exploded through the broken window. The fire had spread to the main room.

"Gigi!" He didn't stop to think or plan, just boosted himself through the window feet-first like she had, managing to avoid the worst of the jagged points in a practiced move from another lifetime.

"Matt! Over here!"

He landed, crouched low and cursed viciously when he saw that she was down, pinned beneath a chunk of counter that had shifted when part of the roof caved in. The fire hadn't yet reached that far, leaving her in a small pocket of safety.

A small and rapidly diminishing pocket.

His mind spun and panic threatened, but he pushed through it and bolted for her, dodging a burning beam and stretching over the tilted counter to yank a small extinguisher from its wall rack.

"Cover your eyes!" When she complied, he hit several small hot spots near her with short blasts of the extinguisher, adding powdery clouds and more smoke to the already foul air.

Coughing, he wedged his shoulder under the edge of the counter and levered it up a few inches. "Go!" He had to bite back a groan when something ripped low down in his left side, where the scar tissue was thick and uncompromising. It burned like hell.

"I'm out!" She dragged herself up, clutching something to her chest.

"Come on!" They staggered toward the window. He boosted her out first. "Run. I'm right behind you."

Of course she didn't go anywhere, damn her, just turned back and reached for him as he came through. Not willing to take any more chances with her, he caught her by the waist, slung her over his shoulder and headed away from the fire.

Her wadded jacket—she went back for her freaking *windbreaker?*—was caught between them as she squirmed and thumped his lower back with her fists, making him wince.

Pissed off and running on way more adrenaline than he wanted to admit, he growled, "Quit it."

"Let me down!"

There was no sign of Bert, but he had moved her vehicle and the three remaining park service Jeeps well out of the range of the fire.

Matt headed toward the cars, dumped her next to her SUV and loomed over her. "What in the *hell* were you thinking, going in there like that?"

She glared right back and opened her mouth to snarl something at him, but he didn't give her a chance. He couldn't listen to an explanation he knew he wouldn't like, couldn't stand the fear and anger, the raging emotions he hadn't felt in years, hadn't ever wanted to feel again.

Overwhelmed with relief that she was okay and fury that she was making him feel things when all he wanted was to be left alone, he closed in on her, used his body to push her up against the SUV. And kissed the hell out of her.

GIGI'S SMARTER SELF would have ducked the kiss, but her smarter self also wouldn't have gone back into a burning building after a piece of evidence.

She almost hadn't made it out.

Blackthorn had saved her life.

Oh, God.

Reaction would set in later, she knew. For now there was only the heat of relief and the pounding burn of adrenaline, which redirected itself the instant his lips touched hers.

The spark that had ignited the first moment she saw him detonated in an instant, decimating her self-control. She gave in to her primal instincts and kissed him back.

He groaned approval and took it deeper.

His mouth seared hers with flames that had nothing to do with arson. He pressed her back against the door of her ride so she felt him, hard and hot and male, with every inch of her body.

Sizzles raced along her skin and beneath it; electricity flowed in her veins and gathered at the points where their bodies aligned.

She gripped his forearms and felt his anger, slid her hands to his shoulders and felt his control slipping. Hers was long gone. She was reckless, wanton, only peripherally aware of the world around them.

The kiss went on and on, until her pulse throbbed and her blood roared in her ears, sounding like the race of an engine.

An engine.

They jerked apart just as headlights speared through the darkness, jolting crazily when the driver gunned the SUV over a hummock.

The vehicle caught air, bounced hard, and swerved into the parking area with a spray of gravel, coming to a rest with its headlights pinned on Gigi. The engine wasn't even fully dead before the doors flew open. Tucker sprang out and rushed toward them with Jack Williams right behind him.

She wasn't sure which was worse: that she had been kissing Blackthorn in the middle of a crisis, or that she resented the interruption. But who would have guessed that Ranger Surly could kiss like that?

Her senses boiled and desire bounded through her with the thick, heavy beat of her heart. She could have died.

Which she hadn't, thanks to him.

The detectives advanced on Blackthorn, who squared off to meet them. He was sweaty and soot-streaked, and his uniform shirt was torn and burned along one side, the skin beneath abraded and angry. And he had lost his hat. Without it, he stopped looking like a cowboy throwback and started looking more like a security professional. Which, she supposed, he was in a way.

"Everyone's out," the ranger reported, voice rasping. Behind him, the station was fully ablaze, sending a thick column of dark smoke into the sky.

Tucker's eyes fixed on Gigi, dark with concern. "You okay?"

She was still pressed flat against her vehicle, and hoped to hell she didn't look as thoroughly kissed as she felt.

Taking a deep breath that did very little to settle the churning in her stomach, she pushed away from the SUV and tried to find some semblance of her professional self.

Looking down, she said, "Well, I think these pants are shot, but the rest of me should be salvageable."

Tucker relaxed a little. "Good to hear. Alyssa made me promise to bring you back down to the city in one piece."

"Then take her with you now and keep her there," Blackthorn said tightly. "She went back into the damn building for her coat."

She rounded on him, arousal souring at the sight of

his face set in hard, uncompromising lines. He was only a few paces away, but it suddenly felt like miles.

And he was trying to get her off the scene. Off the case.

She bristled. "I needed—"

Two low-flying planes roared suddenly overhead, drowning her out. The surrounding rock had shielded their approach, but now amplified the propeller noise as the planes skimmed low and dropped their payloads of gritty reddish fire suppressant.

The first load hit the station, dousing a large portion of the flames. The second painted a barrier line between the fire and the trees immediately downwind, snuffing the few small fires that had been started by flying sparks.

Radio static echoed, and a stocky figure stepped into the distant reaches of the headlight wash to wave at the planes. "Right on target," Bert said into his radio. "Thanks for making the detour."

His voice echoed strangely, coming from the receiver in Tucker's vehicle, but Gigi was reassured by the sound.

They were all out, all okay. That was what mattered. Not the kiss, how much faster Blackthorn had recovered, or the fact that he was trying to get rid of her now.

"Okay, it was a stupid move," she admitted. "But I think you'll agree that the payoff was worth it." Turning to Tucker and Jack, she said, "The guy who knocked me down said something about the fire taking care of 'everything,' which suggests that Tanya got her hands on something they want to keep off the radar. And when I was in her room, I found this hidden in a book."

She scooped her windbreaker up off the ground, dug in the pocket and pulled out the evidence bag holding Tanya's worn sketch. Both the bag and the sketch were worse for wear, but she could still make out the guy sitting in front of the waterfall.

She offered the evidence to Tucker. "Call me crazy, but that looks like Jerry Osage to me."

Osage had been killed during a jailbreak a few years earlier…one that had freed terrorist mastermind al-Jihad and sparked a flurry of terrorist activity in Bear Claw City. Although Osage had seemed to be an innocent by-stander, the new rash of attacks could mean otherwise… And if that was the case, they weren't just dealing with aggravated assault. They might be looking for a terrorist cell.

Chapter Six

Matt cursed under his breath as Tucker took the evidence bag and stared at the sketch, brows drawn together.

Jack looked over his shoulder and whistled. "I'd say Gigi-girl did some serious homework on old cases in Bear Claw."

His too-familiar tone got under Matt's skin the same way Gigi had, leaving him stirred up and pissed off.

Kissing her had been an impulsive move, an effort to burn off some of the fear and frustration that had been riding too high in his bloodstream, but he was the one who'd wound up burned. Her sharp, enticing flavor was branded on his neurons, the feel of her imprinted on every part of his body that had come into contact with hers.

Instead of leveling him off, kissing her had only made things worse.

"It's Osage," Tucker confirmed. "I'd put money on it. If I remember the story right, he moved out here to be with his girlfriend, who was a competitive skier of some sort. We never followed up on her because he looked like collateral damage." He glanced at Gigi. "Impressive."

Her eyes lit a little, but she stayed on task. "Bert

mentioned how most of the rangers who request isolated postings are trying to get away from something."

She walked the detectives through her thought process, but Matt was only half listening, his mind hung up on what Bert had said. Not just because he wondered whether she had asked about him—and, if so, what Bert might have said—but because he wasn't sure he knew the answer anymore.

For a long time, he had believed he came out to Fourteen because out in the backcountry he could contribute without being on the front lines. And because he didn't need anybody but himself.

Over the past few months, though, he had found himself making the trip down into the city more and more often. And feeling restless, edgy, the way he used to get when his subconscious was trying to tell him that he had missed an important connection.

But although he didn't know what he was looking for these days, or what it meant, he knew for damn sure that it wasn't an overly impulsive crime-scene analyst who seemed to want to play cop.

"Good work." Jack gave her a one-armed hug. "I mean it. Seriously impressive."

Matt had to fight not to growl. Or think that the detective would look better without that arm.

She returned the friendly embrace. "The profile was your idea. If you hadn't suggested it, I might've just gone straight home from the crime scene."

If she had, Matt thought, he would have been in the station when the arsonists showed up, and she never would have been endangered. But they also wouldn't have known about the Osage connection, which could prove to be a critical break in the case.

Damn it.

"You going to put together a task force?" Jack asked Tucker.

"That's the chief's call, but we should definitely hit up Fairfax and his people. They're the ones who rooted out the embedded terrorists within the ARX Prison and the Bear Claw P.D. If there's a connection to Osage, they'll find it."

Gigi said, "I'd like to be in on the task force, if there winds up being one."

Jack nodded. "You can ride with me."

Matt's gut churned, especially when Tucker didn't immediately turn down the offer. He cleared his throat. "No offense, but I don't think that's such a good idea."

She flicked him a cool glance. "Prefacing that with 'no offense' doesn't make it any less insulting. Lucky for me, you don't get a vote here."

The fact that he even *wanted* a damn vote went to show how off-track he'd gotten. He turned to Tucker. "You can't seriously be considering this. She's just an analyst."

Jack snorted. "She's also a sniper-level marksman, a seriously dirty street fighter, and a better than decent security-system hacker. She's been doing a couple of ride alongs per week with me, sometimes more."

A pit opened up in Matt's gut. He looked down at her, eyes narrowing. "You've got a badge?"

"Not yet, but I'm working on it." There was a flash of pride beneath her answer. "Denver's piloting an accelerated crisis response program aimed at analysts. I'm in line for one of the first slots."

Crisis response. He wasn't sure if he said the words aloud, or just thought them, but either way they sounded like a curse, and put a nasty, slippery knot in his gut. "You're kidding."

Anger blazed in her eyes, but beneath it, he thought he caught a look of hurt. "I can take care of myself. And what do you care, anyway?"

He didn't. He shouldn't.

"You're right. Sorry." He touched the air near his temple—where the brim of his hat would have been if he hadn't lost it in the fire—and said, "I'll let you guys do the cop thing. Give a shout if you need anything."

Then he turned and headed for where Bert was organizing the volunteers into teams to search the surrounding scrub for hot spots.

They all had jobs to do, and he had come out to Station Fourteen precisely to avoid conversations—and frustrations—like this.

GIGI WOKE UP THE NEXT morning with the bedclothes tangled around her legs, her lips tingling and her mind awash in half-remembered dreams of glittering green eyes.

Banishing the memories—and the warm churn they brought—she blinked at her surroundings. The short-term rental had come furnished in Early Ski Bum, complete with old wooden poles tacked on the wall. Some days she woke up, looked around and thought, *What am I doing here?*

Today was one of those days. She liked Bear Claw well enough, but she wasn't much of a skier.

Unlike Tanya, she thought, who appeared to have quit after Jerry Osage's death.

That was enough to get her up and moving. But it also got her thinking again about the fire. And Blackthorn.

She had held herself together until she got home last night and then let herself have a good cry, needing to get the fear and the shakes out of her system so she would be clear-headed today.

In the light of day, though, it was even more patently obvious that she had been dumb.

Yeah, she'd gained major points with the cops by making the Jerry Osage connection, but that didn't change the fact that she had been reckless, maybe even showing off a bit. And she could have died. Probably would have if Blackthorn hadn't come after her.

The idea of being killed in the line wasn't a new concept. She wasn't stupid; she knew what she was getting into in fighting for a place in hazardous response.

But on a response team, she would be working with the best available information and wearing serious protective gear. And, most importantly, she wouldn't be working solo. She would have a team surrounding her, or at the very least a partner to watch her back.

A partner would have been scouting the bunkhouse while she went through Tanya's room; a partner would have noticed the men outside and sounded the alarm, and the fire never would've gotten started.

And a partner wouldn't have pinned her against her ride and kissed her to the point that her priorities flew right out of her head.

Which she so couldn't think about right now.

Instead, she headed for the P.D. and let herself into the basement complex that housed Bear Claw's crime lab.

She was early enough that she had assumed she would be the first one in, but Alyssa was already in the outer office, hammering away at one of the computer stations.

Bear Claw's head analyst scowled. "I thought I told you to take the day off. Go home."

Gigi returned the frown. "I thought I came here to fill in for Maya so you could take it easy while Baby McDermott gestates. Go home yourself."

"I'm not the one who nearly got crispy crittered yesterday."

"I…" Realizing she wasn't as steady as she had thought, Gigi held up a hand. "Give me a couple of hours before we talk about it, okay? I need some time to process."

Process evidence. Process events. Think about that damned kiss.

She traded her light, subtly studded blazer for her lab coat and headed for the inner lab door. And she felt Alyssa's worried eyes follow her as she pushed through into the first of the lab's interconnected rooms.

The main space housed workbenches, hulking machines, and a row of evidence lockers. On the far side, an airlocked door led to the "clean" rooms, where the more technical procedures—DNA testing, chromatography and other assays—were carried out under negative pressure, fume hoods and other fail-safes.

The whole place was well-lit, painted a creamy white,

and hung with brightly colored posters and prints that ranged from the ridiculous to the macabre. But as far as Gigi was concerned, it still felt like a basement. And for a second, she really, really wanted to be back in her Denver lab, with its wide windows and view of the mountain-flanked city.

Or, better yet, on a deserted tropical island with a lifetime supply of Twix, Caesar salads with full-fat dressing and movies on demand.

Might have to rethink Bert's whole "get away from the world" theory. She was a social creature by nature, but certain topics made her want to head for unoccupied territory. Having people worried about her was one of them.

She got that caring for someone and worrying about them went together. Her mom was six years cancer-free, but Gigi still got nervous when recheck time came around. And she'd found herself watching Alyssa too closely at times over the past few weeks, her instincts pinging a warning every time she thought the mother-to-be might be overexerting herself.

When it came to her work, though, friends and family worrying about her too often made her feel like they didn't think she was good enough to do the job. She had worked her butt off learning to fight harder and shoot better than the other people in the running for the accelerated program, but her family thought it was a phase, and a good chunk of her coworkers still looked at her and saw a lab rat who dressed with a bit of flair.

Or, as in Blackthorn's case, a city slicker who didn't belong anywhere near the backcountry. Even once she'd proved to him that she could hold her own, he'd wanted to shut her out of the action.

She looked around and scowled at the realization that she was exactly where he wanted her—shut up in the lab while he and his rangers searched the foothills. But logically, she could be more use here than there. For the moment, anyway.

So she got to work.

Cassie had collected physical evidence from Tanya at the hospital and started running it last night—the rape kit didn't show any evidence of sexual assault, but there had been some skin under the ranger's fingernails, and she'd had a few defensive wounds. The DNA was processing and Cassie had printed out photos of Tanya— mostly close-ups of her injuries—and stuck them on the magnetic wipe board, where they joined a copy of the Jerry Osage sketch and some earlier, candid photos of Tanya.

Gigi took a long look at Tanya's face in the hospital photos—still pretty and patrician beneath the narrow bruise running along her jaw and the gash on her opposite temple. Then her hands, which were bruised along the knuckles, and splinted at one thumb. Her nails were short and neat, practical. And she had fought back.

That resonated. But it was the last picture in the line that had Gigi pausing. It was a middle-distance shot taken through the door into Tanya's hospital room. A uniformed officer sat by the door, but it was the man inside the room who was the focus of the shot. Cassie had caught Jim Feeney perched on the edge of a visitor's chair, with most of his body angled over Tanya as he held her hand in both of his. Although his face was partly turned away from the camera, the edge of his profile read "grief" and the set of his jaw conveyed "I'm going to stay for as long as it takes"…but the weary lines of his rangy body said he wasn't sure his being there was going to make a difference.

Gigi touched the picture and swallowed to loosen her too-tight throat.

Initially, she had been committed to the case because she was committed to every case that came through her hands, especially when it was a violent crime. More, the victim was a woman close to her age, working in a male-dominated field. There was kinship there. Sympathy.

Another layer had been added when she tangled with Blackthorn, making her determined to show him what she was capable of.

Now, though, she shifted all the way onto the treacherous footing of involvement…which could either help or hinder an analyst.

Usually, with her, it helped.

"So get to work," she told herself.

In the evidence locker, she hesitated over the pencil sketch of Jerry Osage, but decided to wait on processing it. Copies had been sent around, and the rangers were going to check out a couple of the depleted waterfalls in their sectors and see if they could match the background, but she had a feeling they had gotten what they were going to get out of the sketch.

Tanya's clothing was bagged and tagged, as were the hikers' duds, but Tanya had been moved around so much that trace was likely to be a nightmare, and the hikers were incidental. Of the stuff Gigi herself had collected at the scene, there were really only two things that sparked her instincts: the feather and the radio.

She started with the radio, on the theory that if Tanya had been attacked somewhere else, the radio smashed there, then her attackers had probably been the ones to move it. Which might mean they had handled it, maybe even left a print or two.

An hour later, though, she didn't have much. She had gotten three smudged partials that matched Tanya's prints, a couple of hits for each of the other rangers—which was consistent with what Blackthorn had said about the radios being up for grabs—and one really smeared thumb print that didn't belong to any of them, but had retained almost zero detail. She could make out part of one whorl and guess at a couple of the other landmarks, but it wouldn't hold up to any sort of database search.

That was usually the score when it came to crime-scene analysis: five percent big foam fingers, ninety-five percent packing peanuts.

"Let's see if the tech-heads can make anything out of you," she said to the smashed radio. "Maybe they can resuscitate you and get your GPS to cough up something interesting." She rebagged it, put her name on the next line down, and logged it back into the evidence locker.

Then she went for the bag with Blackthorn's shirt in it. And caught herself hesitating.

For crap's sake, Lynd, it's just a shirt. You can process it without picturing him naked. Half naked. Whatever.

She did her best, anyway. It helped that Blackthorn

had ended the evening by trying to run her off the case again. It was really too bad the fates had matched such a truly excellent body with that superior—and totally annoying—attitude.

Remembering his look of horror when he'd heard she wanted to be a critical response cop made it easier to pull the uniform shirt out of the bag, spread it out and start going over it, working her way toward the chest pocket.

His name tag was still in place, the engraved letters spelling out *Matthew H. Blackthorn*. She spent way too much effort not staring at it and wondering about the *H*. Under other circumstances, it would have made her nervous to realize how much she was thinking about him. As it was, she gave herself a pass and called it what it was: a defense mechanism.

If she was thinking about Blackthorn's great ass and borderline personality, she didn't have to think about the fire...or worry about how she was going to smooth things over with Alyssa.

They were good friends and clicked on a level that Gigi didn't connect with many other people on, but now they were heading square into an argument they had skirted around once or twice before, knowing they weren't going to agree.

She was just teasing the feather out of the shirt pocket when the door swung open and Alyssa came through, expression set. She was moving slowly in the final week or so of her pregnancy, but that only added to the impression that she was, in her own way, as much of an immovable force as her husband.

Gigi could be a solid wall when she needed to,

though. And if her family hadn't managed to get her to stick with the lower-risk analyst's position, her new best friend didn't have a prayer.

Alyssa lowered herself to a swivel chair, put her feet on the waist-high desk that ran the perimeter of the room, folded her hands atop the curve of her belly…and fixed Gigi with a look. "Officially, I'm impressed with the drive and dedication you showed last night. That will go in your file. Unofficially, though, I've decided that being your friend isn't for the faint of heart." She paused, and a crack of hurt and concern showed through. "What were you *thinking,* Gigi? You could've died."

"I know that." She met Alyssa's baffled stare. "But right then, all I was thinking about was getting that sketch. It was evidence, and my job is to collect the evidence, period. Not to mention that 'identify the goal and go for it' is pretty much a family motto." She tried a smile. "I think it got cribbed by a sneaker company in edited form: *Just do it.*"

"This isn't a joke, damn it. How do you think I felt, sitting down here while Tucker blasted up into the park, with no clue whether you were okay or not? And then to find out what you *did* do? God." She knotted her fingers together. "I was up half the night thinking about what it would've been like to have you lying in a hospital bed like Tanya, or worse."

"Sorry." The word was an automatic knee-jerk response, but Gigi followed it up with, "Seriously, I'm sorry. I know you care, and I…" She was going to say "I appreciate your concern," but that was a total brush-off line and Alyssa deserved better. The thing was, she *did* appreciate the concern…but it also made her feel squirrelly and trapped, made the basement walls seem suddenly closer than they had been last week, or even an hour ago.

"You can't promise to stay out of trouble," Alyssa finished for her, "because you're hardwired to play hero."

"I'm not playing anything," she said, trying to make her friend understand. "This is my *life* we're talking about—not just the safety part of it, but the living part of it, too. If I compromise on this, I'm giving up part of what makes me…*me*."

"I just want you to be a little more careful. You admit that going back into the station was stupid, right?"

"Now? Yes. But that doesn't happen often." And there had been extenuating circumstances. Distractions in the form of one Matthew H. Blackthorn. She didn't say that, though, partly because she didn't want to go there, and partly because it was no excuse. There would always be distractions during a crisis. "The thing is, I can't promise that I won't make the same mistake again." She paused, trying to choose words that would get across to Alyssa something she hadn't yet gotten even her family to understand. "If I get picked for the program and make it through the training—"

"You mean 'when.' Because if you're not at the top of the list, your bosses in Denver are a bunch of idiots."

"Okay, 'when' I get on a team, my teammates are going to be depending on me to react appropriately, no matter what's going on around me. And although there's lots more sitting-and-waiting-and-planning than you'd think, there will also be times that I'm going to need to prioritize the job over my own safety. I'm not stupid and I'm not suicidal…but I can't be as cautious as the people who care about me want me to be."

People like Alyssa and her other analyst friends, who didn't get why she needed to escape from pure after-the-fact labwork. And like her mother and sisters, who still sent her job listings from their universities, somehow thinking that teaching and doing were the same thing.

"Are you sure the program is going to be right for you?"

"Of course."

"Why?"

"What do you mean, 'why?'" Gigi would have rolled her eyes, but she didn't want to minimize Alyssa's concerns—she just wanted to get at something. Choosing her words carefully, she said, "I want to get into the program because the members of the hazardous response teams are the ultimate cops, and their work is the ultimate adrenaline rush." Which wasn't far off from the answer she had given the selection committee during her interview. More, it was the truth. Her parents had given her every opportunity to excel, and she intended to do exactly that. Maybe not the way they had intended, but still.

"And you're happiest when you're the ultimate?"

"It's not about being happy or unhappy, it's about establishing myself. Once I've done that, then I can think about the other stuff in life—a husband, family, that sort of thing." But that rang false, and honesty forced her to add, "Not that I'm likely to do the family thing if I'm with HRT. Not many guys can deal with having a wife who's right out on the front lines."

"Especially one who'd jump back into a burning

building because she forgot her jacket." But Alyssa paused, then shook her head. "I think you'd be surprised. More guys than you might imagine are okay with stuff like that. Or at least some of them can get themselves square with it if that's what it takes to make things work." She sent a speculative look. "Tucker said Matt was pissed about you going back in there."

"I can't totally blame him. He was the one who had to carry me out."

Whether thanks to hormones or a shared desire not to turn this into a friendship-leveling fight, Alyssa let herself be diverted. Unfortunately, she veered in a direction Gigi had been hoping to avoid. "He *carried* you?"

Gigi flushed and focused on the feather, dropping it into the bottom half of a plastic Petri dish and slipping it into position beneath the bright field of a light microscope. "He was probably just making sure I didn't double back again."

But Alyssa wasn't buying it. "Tucker said there were vibes. What's going on with you two?"

"Me and Tucker? Nothing, I swear."

"Ha ha. Very funny. Spill."

"There's nothing *to* spill." At least nothing she was ready to talk about. "Blackthorn is rude, temperamental, arrogant, cynical and…" She trailed off because that wasn't fair. He was all of those things, yes, but he was also tough, capable and fiercely committed to his job and the people who worked for him.

"And?"

"And I'm not interested." Gigi made a few notes, switched the scope from 100x to 400x and looked again. No big foam finger yet.

"There's a difference between 'not interested' and 'don't want to be interested.'"

"Fine. I don't want to be interested. Aside from the know-it-all attitude, the guy's got some pretty serious layers, and I'm not into layers. I prefer men where what you see is what you get."

Alyssa made a "no kidding" face, but then sobered. "I could tell you about a couple of those layers if you want."

She hesitated, but shook her head. "No. Don't." She had her path charted, her goals set. A pleasant detour was one thing. A cross-country trip on dirt roads without a map or GPS was another. The first one was fun. The second could go really wrong.

Increasing the magnification another notch, she got up close and personal with some little alien-type creatures that were crawling on the feather. *Ew.*

Alyssa pressed further. "Look, Tucker has known Matt a long time, and says he's never seen him act the way he was acting last night over you. And maybe I haven't known you all that long, but I've never seen you do the verbal duck-and-weave like this before. That tells me there's something there…or could be."

"No." Gigi shook her head. "I'm sorry, but no. The timing is…well, it's wrong. That's all."

"You're the one who pointed out that moving back to Denver wasn't the same as taking a trip to Mars."

"It's not the logistics, it's…" Everything. She made another note, caught herself looking at the shiny name tag again. "You know how I've told you about how my family lives life full blast? Well, the same thing goes in the relationship department. It's all or nothing.

Consuming. The emotions…there's no room left for anything else except the emotions. And when it crashes, the debris field goes on for miles." She couldn't risk something like that. Not when she was so close to nailing a slot in the accelerated program.

Alyssa narrowed her eyes. "Who was he?"

"What are you, an analyst or something?" But Gigi lifted a shoulder. "It doesn't matter. It was a long time ago." She could barely picture him now, in fact. All she knew was that for one glorious, tumultuous summer during college, he had been her whole universe. And when he left, she had crashed hard, nearly washing out of her senior year in the process. She had graduated, but had been the only one of her four sisters to miss getting summa cum laude honors. "What matters is that I let everything else around me take a backseat to a guy, and I can't afford to do that right now."

Maybe not ever. Miserable wasn't a good color on her.

"I think first love is supposed to be awful like that," Alyssa pointed out. "You're all grown up now. It'll feel different."

"Yeah. It's worse. After Matt kissed me—" She broke off.

"Hel-lo. He *kissed* you?" Alyssa's feet thumped to the floor. "Was this before or after he carried you out of a burning building?"

Gigi pressed a gloved hand to her lab-coat-covered stomach in a gesture that did zilch to settle the jitters. "After. I dreamed about him last night."

What was it about him? He wasn't anything like the men she usually gravitated toward. *Opposites might attract,* her grandmother liked to say, *but they don't stick for the long haul.* Was this some sort of belated teenaged rebellion on the part of her subconscious? Had her hormones latched on to him because, like her job choices, he went against the grain? She didn't have a clue.

All she knew was that even though he had done his Ranger Surly routine last night, the thought of him still sent hot and cold shivers racing through her body. And that, more than anything, warned her that there wasn't any sort of compromise to be had. She couldn't get involved with him partway, couldn't have the sort of "just having fun" interlude that had once been as natural to her as breathing.

"I can't go there," she said, more to herself than to Alyssa. "I'm on the verge of my big break. I need to concentrate on that. Besides, even if I were inclined to get involved with someone right now—which I'm not—I need someone who respects my career choices. Which he doesn't. He made that perfectly clear last night."

"About that—" Alyssa began, but the ring of the lab's landline interrupted her. She checked the display, and her expression softened as she answered, "Hello, Mc-Dermott, Homicide. What's the word?" She listened for a second before her expression shifted. "Really? Wow. Okay. Come on down."

Gigi went on alert. "What's going on?"

"The P.D. is forming a new task force, and I've been officially asked to release you to them for the time being. You and your new partner will both be deputized for the duration."

The words banged around in Gigi's head for a

moment, refusing to compute. She was thrilled about being tapped for the task force, but… "What do you mean, deputized? And what new partner? I ride with Jack."

"Not anymore you don't," an all-too-familiar voice said from the doorway behind her.

She froze. Oh, no. Tucker hadn't. He wouldn't.

Would he?

The look Alyssa sent her—part sympathy, part dare—said that he would, and he had.

Gigi's body washed hot, then cold, then back to hot again. She turned slowly, not ready to face Blackthorn, especially not now, when her usual defenses were gone, stripped away by girl talk.

But there he was, and she was going to have to deal with him. And with the way her body lit up at the sight of him filling the doorway. His presence seemed larger somehow down here in the rapidly shrinking confines of the basement.

Heat speared through her, tempting and tantalizing, and making her think of hot sheets and waking with his taste on her lips.

Maybe her awareness was so thoroughly heightened because she knew him now, had kissed him, been kissed by him. Or maybe it was the jeans and short-sleeved white button-down he wore in place of his tan-and-green uniform, making him look different, somehow less aloof.

But then he shifted away from the doorframe, and her eyes zeroed in on his worn leather belt. Or, rather, on the badge and holster that rode together on his left hip.

Deputized, Alyssa had said, which accounted for the

badge, with its familiar Bear Claw P.D. insignia. But that didn't explain why the holster bore LAPD markings… or why, when he saw her staring, his expression went brittle and he looked away.

Gigi's instincts fired in all directions, telling her something big was going on, but not what, or how she was supposed to handle it.

In the end, she said, stupidly, "But you're a ranger."

He looked back at her, one corner of his sculpted mouth kicking up with zero amusement. "I am now. Before that, I had a decade on the job. Now I guess I'm doing an encore, thanks to budget cuts and the fact that Tucker knew I was going to be working this case with or without sanction." But his expression said that was only half of the story.

She had a feeling she knew the rest. "I don't need a babysitter."

"Nobody said you did. And speaking of babies…" He looked past her to Alyssa and mock-glared. "I thought you were supposed to be taking it easy."

Hello, subject change. Gigi didn't know what to make of that, what to make of any of it. But she couldn't take her eyes off his weapon, which was an older Sig Sauer, a warhorse of an automatic.

"My darling wife is *supposed* to be on her way home," Tucker said, coming up behind Blackthorn to shoot Alyssa a stern look.

"I'm sitting," she said primly, but with a "don't push me" look in her eyes. "So catch me up. Where do we stand on the Jerry Osage connection?"

Gigi only half listened as Tucker summarized what his contacts had come up with so far, which was that yes,

Jerry's murder had been the catalyst for Tanya packing up her skis and becoming a ranger, but no, there didn't seem to be any connection between the two cases. "Nobody's taking any bets, though," he said, "which is why we're mobilizing a joint task force with the park service, including our newest deputies." He raised an eyebrow in Gigi's direction. "You on board? Ready to get deputized so you and your partner can head out?"

Deputized. Partner. This wasn't happening.

Was it?

Her better sense screamed for her to take a second to think it through, turn it down. There was no way in hell she and Blackthorn would survive being partnered up. He was going to try to rein her in, marginalize her, and she was going to be tempted to be twice as reckless as usual just to prove she could.

But she nodded to Tucker. "Lay it on me."

Because, really, there was no way she could turn down the opportunity. It meant she would be working the case on an official basis while shadowing a ten-year veteran of the LAPD. It was going to look great on her résumé. As for the rest of it…well, she would deal. She was a Lynd, she could handle anything.

Besides, maybe she would get lucky. Maybe he'd be such a jerk that her blossoming crush would wither and die.

"Here. Catch." Tucker tossed her a badge like the one Blackthorn wore on his belt: a Bear Claw P.D. shield with the serial number blank.

She snagged it on the fly, and took a deep breath to settle the sudden churn of excitement in her belly as Tucker led her through an abbreviated swearing-in and ran through what she could and couldn't do out in the field. "As for the rest of it," he finished, "just ask Captain Blackthorn here, former leader of SWAT Team Four out of East L.A."

Gigi's heart *thudda-thudded* and the bottom dropped out of her stomach, as though she had suddenly jumped onto an elevator headed straight up into the stratosphere. She stared at Blackthorn as a whole lot of clues suddenly lined up.

Blackthorn was SWAT, or had been. Not only that, he had been a team leader. The best of the best.

His face darkened. "Seriously, McDermott, don't call me that. And if you value your face, you won't get anyone *else* doing it, either." He glanced over at Gigi, though she couldn't read much in his expression.

She sucked in a shaky breath. "Blackthorn, I—"

"Call me Matt already," he interrupted. "Not Blackthorn. Not ranger. And not captain anything. Just Matt. Got it?"

She nodded, but wasn't capable of coherent speech as her brain finally assembled the four critical new facts and entered them into evidence:

Fact one: Blackthorn—or, rather, Matt—was a former über-cop.

Fact two: he outranked her. Even if she aced the accelerated program, it would be years before she could shoot for captain. And although logic said his old rank shouldn't matter here and now, it did.

Fact three: he looked incredible in street clothes, and he wore his gun and badge like they were a part of him that had been missing.

Fact four: she was in serious trouble. Because if there

was one thing a Lynd woman liked better than being the best at what she did, it was meeting a man who was even better.

Chapter Seven

Within about a minute of walking into the lab, Matt had decided that if Gigi at full throttle had put a serious scare in him, she was even more terrifying when shocked into silence. Worse, she was staring at him like he'd just grown a second head…or thrown a cape over his shoulders and whipped off his shirt again, this time to reveal superhero spandex.

Ah, crap. He hadn't seen this one coming. Maybe he should have, but he was seriously rusty on the man-woman stuff. And Gigi was…well, she wasn't like anyone else he'd ever met. Or kissed.

And, yeah, the kiss was going to be a problem; it had been since the moment he'd moved in, his body over-riding his usual survival instincts. He didn't know how much further it would have gone if Tucker hadn't shown up, but the simple kiss had made him all too aware of how damn long it had been for him. She was hot—if unconventional—and he was horny, and he had decided that was a bad combination even before Tucker called to float the idea of them working together.

His first response had been a flat-out "No way in hell!" But Tucker had promised him that Gigi would be gone in thirteen days. The word from her home base was that they would need her one way or the other: either she would be heading for the academy or she would be covering for someone who was.

That was why sometime during the long hours Matt had spent staring at the ceiling of his bedroom, far too aware of Bert tossing and turning on the couch in the main room of his quarters, he had talked himself into going along with Tucker's plan. He had told himself that being deputized would get him smack in the loop, and it would mean he'd be stepping on fewer toes.

Really, though, there was only one real reason he was doing it: to keep Gigi from getting herself killed.

He had sworn off trying to fix people's lives, it was true. But given all the stuff that had gone down in the past twenty-four hours, and the fact that he knew damn well that she was going to keep herself square in the middle of the case, he hadn't been able to walk away. Not from her. Not from Tanya. And not from whatever was going on in his sector.

He could handle himself around Gigi for a couple of weeks. Or so he'd thought. But that was before he'd strapped the gun and badge back on, and things had gotten even weirder.

The moment he'd felt those familiar weights, old feelings came flooding back: the responsibility and connectedness; the knowledge that the whole damn world was riding right over his shoulder, breathing down on him…and the low-grade acid churn that said no matter how good he was, how much he planned things out, plugged gaps and covered contingencies, the odds were that he'd lose someone.

Worse, now Gigi was staring at him like she expected him to leap tall buildings and shoot laser beams from his eyes. Oh, she was trying to hide it, of course, but it was there.

This was a bad idea. He should back out now, head up to the mountains where he belonged, and join one of the search parties.

Or, better yet, go search on his own.

But if he did that, she'd be riding along with Jack Williams, who thought she'd make a hell of a cop.

At the thought, the churn got worse.

"How is this going to work?" she asked him, a reasonable question that put him back in the too-familiar role of calling the shots. He didn't kid himself, though. Soon enough the shock would wear off and the loose cannon would return.

"Security here in the P.D. is going to be ramped up until we know one way or another about the terrorist connection." That was a no-brainer, given that the building itself had been infiltrated once before. "But any time you want to be out in the field, you'll hit me up and we'll make arrangements to meet."

Her eyes narrowed. "News flash. You're supposed to be my partner, not my bodyguard."

"I'm the one with the gun." He patted his hip, wishing he had his damn shotgun instead. And wishing that the Sig didn't feel like such an old friend.

She rolled her eyes. "Hello? Sharpshooter here. My ACP is in my locker and I'm licensed to carry concealed."

"Hell." This just got better and better.

"If I could interject?" Alyssa said drily.

"Only if you're going to tell her not to go out without backup."

Gigi's expression went smug. "She's seen me shoot. The only time I hit the granny cutout was when I meant to. And I called it first."

"Which isn't the same thing as taking down another human being. Especially one that's shooting back and aiming to kill."

She didn't have a comeback for that one, just scowled at him.

"He's right," Alyssa said, "and what's more, you know it. Or you would if you took a breath and chilled for a second." Gigi transferred her glare, but Alyssa just blinked unperturbed, and continued, "Regardless of whether or not Tanya's attack and the arson were committed by al-Jihad's people, the cases are clearly connected to each other."

Tucker stepped in. "Gigi's attacker wanted to destroy something. Maybe there's a drug connection? There's been some buzz lately about a new product on the streets, and there have been a couple of really weird ODs." He paused. "And let's not forget about all those break-ins up at the upper-level ranger stations over the past few months. They could fit in somehow, too."

"Huh," Matt said. He hadn't gone there, but Tucker was right. It played.

"Whoever these guys are, and whatever they're after," Tucker continued, "the one Gigi saw has got to be seriously stressed."

Gigi scowled. "Having Alyssa do a detailed sketch of the back of his head isn't going to get us anywhere."

"He doesn't know that's all you saw, and the fire

made it on the news, so they probably know that you survived. Are you willing to bet they're not going to come after you to finish the job?"

"We could use me to lure—"

"Like hell," Matt growled over Tucker's calmer "Let's hold off on that."

Gigi drew breath to argue, but Alyssa lurched to her feet, getting their attention in a hurry. To Gigi, she said, "I want you to promise me you'll let the P.D. protect you. No sneaking off, and no ditching your backup. If you don't want to work with Matt, I'm sure Jack will trade."

"Hold on a minute—" Matt began.

"No, you hold on." To his surprise, Alyssa rounded on him, eyes stormy. "I don't care what you and Tucker cooked up. Gigi is my analyst, and she's right, I've seen her shoot. She's good. Better than good. In fact, she's good at just about everything she tries. She's also one of the most intuitive analysts I've ever worked with. Which means she doesn't need a babysitter—she needs someone who'll give her room to do her job. If you can't do that, whether because of your history, or because of what is or isn't going on between the two of you, then you need to step aside. I will *not* run the risk of someone getting hurt because you're wrangling when you should be watching out for each other."

Gigi's wince was almost comical. Almost.

Matt gritted his teeth, but Alyssa was right, he was riding on adrenaline and emotion, and that wasn't going to do any of them any good. He needed to get a freaking grip, and he needed to do it now. Because handing

Gigi off to Williams might make sense, but he couldn't do it.

"You don't have to worry about me," he said, flinching when he heard the words come out in his crisis-mode voice: calm and level, a total lie that covered up the other stuff inside. "Your call, Greta Grace."

He saw Alyssa mouth, *Greta Grace?* but kept his eyes locked on Gigi.

She made a face. "You call me that again, and I'll 'Captain Blackthorn' you so fast it'll make your head spin."

"Noted." But something inside him uncoiled a notch. "So we're good? Partners?" He thought about holding out a hand to shake, but stuck his thumbs in his belt loops instead.

"I don't know if I'd call us 'good,'" she said, voice going wry, "but yeah, partners. Largely because I need a bird expert, and I'd probably have to ask you for an intro anyway. You being a ranger and all."

"I already gave a buddy over at the university a heads up that we'd be there right after lunch." At her look, he shrugged. "The feather was in *my* shirt." And he'd been planning on working the case with or without a badge. Or a partner.

"Fine. Ready when you are." Gigi avoided his eyes as she moved past him to grab a fresh evidence bag and tweeze the feather into it.

"And you promise not to ditch him?" Alyssa pressed. When Gigi hesitated, she made big, mournful eyes. "You wouldn't want your oh-so-pregnant friend to spend another sleepless night worrying about you, right?"

Gigi winced. "No fair."

"I mean it."

"Okay. I swear. Pinkie swear, even." She sealed and signed the evidence bag, then slanted a look in Matt's direction. "Aren't you going to make him promise?"

"I'm not worried about him."

Maybe you should be, he thought. Not because he would ditch his partner, but because he wasn't in the zone anymore. And even when he had been, he'd failed, badly. But there was no point in bringing that up now, so he tipped his head toward the door. "Come on, partner. Let's go see a man about a feather."

She hooked the badge on her belt, tucked away the evidence bag, exchanged a few words with Alyssa about other pieces of evidence, and headed for what looked like a break room, calling over her shoulder, "Let me just grab my gun and we can go."

He winced, but didn't argue.

PARTNERS, GIGI THOUGHT, fighting not to hang on to the door handle as Matt sent his Jeep hurtling through the city like a madman.

A day ago, she would've thought he was driving like he was in the backcountry, heedless of traffic and signs. Now, though, she knew better: he was driving like he had a siren and wig-wag lights going, and he was hustling his team to a crisis call.

His jaw was set, his knuckles white, his bearing screamed *cop*...and her stomach was knotted with a mix of nerves and desire.

This was the guy she had seen last night when he was organizing the search, the one who blew her away, turned her on. Where Ranger Blackthorn had tried to lose himself in isolation, Captain Blackthorn was right there with her. And he was hurting.

He had fled to the backcountry to escape something that happened while he was on the job, she realized now. More than the scars, this was the unhealed wound.

"So," she said when he seemed content with silence. "What made you leave L.A.?"

He cut her a dark look. "Could we not do this right now?"

She knew she could run a Google search for it, but she wanted to hear it from him. Not just because it would be coming from the perspective of a team leader—a goal she hadn't yet even really admitted to herself—but because...well, because. "When, then?"

"Later."

"Which really means never."

"It means later. I say what I mean."

She thought about it, realized he'd withheld information, but never actually lied to her, at least not that she knew. "Fair enough. I can be patient."

He snorted, but the air lightened between them. A few blocks later, he unbent enough to say, "The arson investigators confirmed that they used Molotov cocktails in the bedrooms and kitchen, and gas around the exterior."

Her stomach gave a low-grade twinge, but she said only, "I keep trying to figure out what they were trying to get rid of. Whatever it was, either Tanya hid it well, or it wasn't in her bedroom."

"If it was in the station, it's gone now." He paused. "Maybe they just wanted to wipe out her connection to Jerry."

Which brought them back to the terrorists. "How would they know to look for that sketch? And why now?"

"No clue. And given that the search hasn't turned up Tanya's Jeep, never mind any radio parts, we probably won't know unless she wakes up." He took a corner so fast that the outside edge of the Jeep got light. Cursing under his breath, he got the vehicle back in line, and eased off on the gas. "Sorry."

Her fingers dug into the door handle, but she kept her voice mild. "Just get us there alive and without collateral damage, and we'll call it even."

She didn't blame him for being angry, would've respected him less if he hadn't been. And she already respected him far too much.

He fell silent, but kept the Jeep within ten of the legal limit for the rest of the drive out to the sprawling U.C. Bear Claw campus, where he weaved through interconnecting roads, bumped the vehicle up onto the curb in front of a big stone building and killed the engine in a No Parking zone.

His slanted look dared her to comment, but she just climbed out, plenty used to city cops in "get it done" mode. And as they headed up the stone steps of a big, museum-like building, walking shoulder-to-shoulder, she realized she was relating to him better on that level than she had as a ranger.

Up in the backcountry, he had stared off into the distance as he had watched over her, standing motionless on the ridgeline. Here at the outskirts of the city, he watched the corners and shadows and stayed on the move. His energy was different now—edgy and restless.

"Tell me about your bird guy," she said as they passed beneath a sign that read "Absalom Center of Environmental Studies" and went into the building.

"Ian Scott. He's a friend."

He said it simply, but she had a feeling there weren't many people he considered friends. Tucker, maybe. "Did you meet him rangering?"

"In college." He ignored her sidelong look and turned down a wide, waxed hallway that was weekend-empty, though the building had the faint vibe of life that said it wasn't totally deserted. "We had some classes together back in the day."

"Was he why you picked Bear Claw?"

"No. Maybe. I don't know." He pushed open a glass door with "Ornithology" stenciled in black. "What matters right now is that he's our best bet for a quick ID on that feather."

It all matters, she thought as she preceded him into an open office space that had a seemingly random assortment of cubicles, bird posters on the walls and the distinctive airlock door that led to a working lab.

The tall spider of a man who unfolded from behind a cluttered desk surprised Gigi. He wore jeans, rope sandals and a T-shirt with a picture of a big black bird, wings outstretched, that invited her to "hang with a cormorant," whatever that meant. His mid-brown hair brushed his shoulders and he had an abstract tribal tattoo encircling his throat.

Gigi liked him at first sight.

"Blackie!" He came toward them, arms outstretched

to first pump Matt's hand and then enfold him in a back-thumping hug. "It's about time you came down off that mountain of yours."

To her surprise, Matt returned a couple of shoulder slaps before he drew away. "Hey. I like my mountain."

"Not enough birds." As the ornithologist pulled back, he looked past Matt's shoulder and saw her, and his dark blue eyes lit appreciatively. "But who needs a flock when one will do nicely?" He held out a hand, as much inviting her into their familiar circle of two as he was offering to shake. "Dr. Ian Scott, at your service. But you'll call me Ian, of course."

"Gigi Lynd, CSI." She took his hand, let his fingers enfold hers and draw her closer.

"Sit, please." He scooped a pile of books off a visitor's chair with one hand, keeping hold of her with the other. "You're a crime scene analyst? Fascinating. I love the shows, you know."

She sat, perversely enjoying Matt's low growl. "Don't believe everything you see on TV. Those shows are more fiction than fact sometimes. Given the level of specialization required in the lab these days, lots of analysts are hired for their science backgrounds, not because they're cops. The TV shows tend to combine real jobs to make things more interesting."

"Of course," he said cheerfully. "Just like movie science. Total crap, but entertaining despite—and sometimes because of—the fact." Leaving Matt to roll his own chair from behind a computer workstation on the other side of the room, Ian sat back down at his desk opposite her, eyes gleaming. "So. Blackie said you have a feather?"

"Yes. How much has, um, Blackie told you?"

Matt put his chair beside hers, sat too close and leaned in to say under his breath, "You sure you want to go there, *Greta?*"

Resisting the organic, almost animalistic temptation to lean into him, she made herself straighten away instead. But her blood hummed and her skin prickled, brought alive by his nearness. Which was so not cool.

Ian answered, "He told me that you needed help IDing some evidence. Because I don't shut myself up in the middle of nowhere, and therefore have some knowledge of current affairs, I assume it has something to do with the ranger who was attacked, and the subsequent torching of Matt's station."

Despite the quips she saw the underlying concern, the quick shift of his eyes toward Matt and away, as if making sure he was really there, really okay.

How long had it been since they had last seen each other? Had Matt left behind not just his career in L.A., but his family and friends, as well? How many more layers were there?

"The ranger who was attacked was clutching the thing when she was found. I know my bird basics, but I didn't recognize it." Matt glanced at her. "Did you get anything off it?"

She reached into the inner pocket of her jacket for the flat carrying case. "There wasn't any obvious trace or transfer, and so far, all I've come up with is that it's not synthetic, hasn't been sterilized for commercial use and probably came from a living bird relatively recently. The mites I saw under magnification were still alive, at any rate." She slid the evidence bag across the table.

Ian waggled his finger. "Mites are resilient buggers. They can go for weeks, months, even years on just—" He broke off with a strangled noise, face draining of color. Almost hesitantly, he used one finger to pull the bag closer, then leaned in to inspect the strangely striped feather. "Holy. Crap."

Gigi's heart thudded in her chest and she nearly shot to her feet and punched the air. Finally, it looked like they had caught a break!

"Where was your ranger found?" Ian's voice was cathedral-hushed.

Matt had gone very still, his expression wary, as if he didn't want to get ahead of himself over something that might be nothing. "About an hour northwest of the station house. I take it we've got something here?"

"I'll say." Ian tapped the edge of the bag, well away from the feather itself. "This is…wow. Unexpected. It's from a barred eagle."

"They're rare?" Gigi pressed.

Ian shook his head and met her eyes, expression lit with wonder. "No, not rare. Completely extinct."

Chapter Eight

Gigi sat back in her chair, stunned. "Extinct?"

"Well, as it's technically defined, anyway. There's no real way to prove that something doesn't exist, you know. The last known breeding population died out in the sixties. At the time, the naturalists blamed pesticides, but the barred eagles stuck to really barren areas at fairly high altitudes, which weren't exactly farming hot spots. The current theory is that they suffered from heavy-metal poisoning. The darn things were attracted to ore sites, mines, that sort of thing, which meant they were probably overexposed to the metals." He paused. "There have been sightings off and on up in the backcountry, but no evidence." He looked back down at the feather, and said softly, "Until now."

"Barred eagles?" Matt muttered. "What is going on? What do they have to do with Tanya?"

"Beats me. I'm just following the evidence." Gigi stared at the bagged feather. How had they gone from terrorists to an extinct species?

She had the sneaking suspicion that this particular piece of evidence could lead them off on a tangent. And even if it was relevant, how could the information possibly help them? It was one thing for the feather to belong to a rare bird that had only a few nesting grounds, thus narrowing down the search for a primary crime scene. It was another thing entirely to go goose-chasing after an ecological ghost.

Matt said, "What if the al-Jihad connection is just a coincidence, and this is the real motive?"

"What, you think Tanya could have crossed paths with someone who wanted to make sure he was the first person to 'rediscover' the barred eagle?" She shook her head. "I don't see the guys who torched your station as ornithologists."

But a glance at Ian made her wonder. He seemed lost in exuberant thought, his eyes gleaming as he muttered to himself, "We need to get in there and confirm, see what we can do about conservation." His hands spasmed, as if he wanted to yank the plume out of the evidence bag, but was holding himself back.

Matt, too, was watching him. "The whole 'publish or perish, you have to be number one or you're nothing' thing can be a powerful motivator."

An inner quiver shook Gigi because that hit close to the bone, but she tried to think it through. Ian had been legitimately shocked at seeing the feather; there was no way he was involved in anything underhanded there. Still, his passion was evident. In another man, it might look a lot like fanaticism…and from there it was often a short fall to violence.

She shook her head. "I don't see this as a battle over who gets bragging rights. For one thing, we're dealing with a whole bunch of guys." Jack and Tucker estimated that it would've taken at least four to lock down the station house so quickly. "And while there have been cases of academic murder…" She shook her head. "It doesn't feel right. But then again, my job is working the evidence. The story is up to the cops and lawyers."

"Yeah, well, today you're on story duty, too."

"An hour northwest of the station house, you said?" Ian asked, seeming to remember they were there.

"Not so fast." Matt held up a hand. "Listen to me, okay? You can't go running off with this feather and start calling in the barred eagle experts, okay? We need to take this slowly."

"Huh? What's wro— Oh." Ian stared at them, his eyes clearing as he refocused, then darkening with understanding. "The feather is still evidence."

Gigi added, "Not only that, but we were hoping it would help lead us to the place where she was attacked." Instead it looked like they were going to have to find the place some other way, and in the process maybe lead Ian to the eagles.

"Can you give us any specifics on where we should be looking?" Matt asked. "High altitudes, you said. How high? And what kinds of ore? I don't know of any copper mines or deposits up near Fourteen, but we could check for surveys."

"Good point," Gigi said. Maybe the evidence wasn't quite played out yet, after all. "What do they eat?"

"I think… Let me see." Ian spun his chair and rolled it to a stuffed-full bookcase along the wall. "Where is… Aha. There you are." Gigi's stomach took a long, slow roll as he pulled out a thin volume. *"Ferrier's Guide to the Flora and Fauna of the Colorado Mountains,"* he announced. "It was the definitive guide back in the day.

Comprehensive, though the organization is seriously wonky. It may take me a minute to find our eagle."

"Look near the back," she said softly. "About three-quarters of the way through."

He shot her a curious look, but complied, then flipped a few more pages and stopped, eyebrows raised. "Well, hello. I guess you didn't need me after all, did you?"

"I didn't know the bird. I knew the book." She met Matt's eyes. "Let's add a waterfall to our list of things to look for." Because the sketch of Jerry Osage sitting in front of a waterfall had been stuck between the pages near the entry for the barred eagle.

Matt leaned in. "What else is listed near there?"

"This is the end of the birds." Ian flipped a few pages. "Then we get into the 'flora' part. Which, for some reason, starts with trees. Specifically those weird pines that grow up near the Forgotten."

Gigi frowned. That was the second time in as many days she'd heard the name. Alyssa had said something about it yesterday. "I assumed that was a ghost story or something. You mean it's a real place?"

"It's both," Matt said. "It's this grim chunk of waste-land that runs along the edge of the park's northwest corner—except for a couple of rivers, it's too dry to support anything but some real scrubby trees and a few coyotes, too far away to be a real tourist draw, and not challenging enough to interest the more extreme hikers. Question is: Would it be barred eagle country?"

Ian shook his head. "Unless they've done some major adapting over the past fifty or so years, the elevation is too high. And there wouldn't be much in the way of food. The place is pretty deserted."

"Is it part of the park?" Gigi asked, trying to figure out where the Forgotten belonged in the puzzle, if at all.

"It's federal land," Matt answered, "but the feds'll never do anything with it, which makes it a perfect buffer for Sector Fourteen."

"Actually, the city bought it from the feds," Ian corrected. "Last I heard, the mayor had nearly managed to pawn it off on a private buyer to help offset budget problems, but there was some holdup over the paperwork. Something about impact statements, I think."

"How long has this been going on?" Matt snapped.

"Six months maybe." Ian sent him a look. "I assumed you knew. As it is, I think it's pretty much a done deal at this point. Just needs the last few rubber stamps."

"Son of a—" Matt broke off, gritting his teeth. "Proudfoot must've made sure word didn't reach me. Probably a deal of some sort with the Park Service so they wouldn't fuss. But Sector Fourteen needs those rivers. Hell, that whole damn side of the park does. If some private buyer starts mucking around up there and screws with the water, the west side will go as dry as the east and it'll all burn."

Gigi said, "If there are already problems with the impact statements, maybe there's still time to make some noise."

Ian shook his head and said, "Proudfoot has it all tied up." He glanced at Matt. "Too bad nobody legitimate stepped up and ran against him, even after the mess he made as acting mayor." His voice was mild, but there was something very far from mild in his expression, and in the way tension suddenly snapped into the air between the two men.

Matt glared at him. "Leave it alone."

"But you could have—"

"Leave. It. Alone."

Gigi did a double take as the conversation veered from the Forgotten to something else entirely. "Wait. What did I just miss?"

"Nothing." Matt tugged on her arm to bring her with him, and said in a suddenly formal, cop-to-civilian expert voice, "Thanks for the help with the feather. We'll let you know if we see the eagle, and if not, when it's safe for your people to come in and search."

Ian rose and came around the desk to put himself between them and the door, eyes firing. "I'm just saying it would've been nice if there had been someone else to vote for. Someone who has a political science degree and used to say he was going to put in his twenty on the force and run for governor, because if an actor could do it, why not a cop?"

Matt's fingers closed tighter on her arm, almost to the point of pain. His face, though, had gone hard and distant. "You should've taken the hint when I ducked all your calls. I'm not that guy anymore. I haven't been in a long time."

"You don't need to be anybody but who you are right now, today," Ian insisted. "The last mayor resigned in the middle of a sex scandal, and Proudfoot is well on his way to running the city into the ground. If someone like you could bring integrity back to the office, it would go a long way to healing—"

"Fine," Matt snapped. "If that's your plan then go

and find someone like me. Because I'm not interested, and I'm not available." He dropped Gigi's arm and headed for the door, leaving her standing there, brain spinning.

This wasn't the ranger's detachment or the cop's intensity she was seeing—this was anger overlain with a deep, restless frustration that was as powerful as it was unfocused.

Ian followed them to the door. "Okay, you're not interested or available. So what are you? Because you sure as hell don't look happy."

Matt stopped and spun back, expression dark. "I'm in the middle of the case from hell. It's not murder yet, but it's only a matter of time before they get brave enough, desperate enough. I've got a ranger in the hospital, another one sleeping on my couch, and I'm wearing a damn badge. So forgive me if I'm not in a very happy place at the moment."

"I'm not talking about right this second and you damn well know it," Ian pressed. "Are you doing what you really want, or is it just easier this way? Tell me you're happy, Blackie, and I'll leave you alone."

Gigi wanted to slip out and let them argue in private, but she couldn't move. Her pulse thudded in her ears.

"I *was* happy, damn it. Forty-eight hours ago, I was just fine. I had air, sunshine, privacy and three good rangers in charge of keeping the hikers from killing themselves. And I'll get back to that peace and quiet when this case is over and life goes back to normal. A week, thirteen days on the outside, and, yeah, I'll be happy again." His voice went harsh. "I just want to be left alone. Is that so damn much to ask?"

"Not if that's what you really want."

"I just said it was, didn't I? Ian, let it go already. And don't call us, we'll call you." Cutting a black look in Gigi's direction, Matt snapped, "Come on. We're leaving." He yanked open the door and stormed out, boots thudding angry beats on the waxed marble, the sound cutting off as the glass door eased shut in his wake.

She didn't follow, just stood staring after him for a moment, stomach roiling in such tight knots that she didn't know whether she wanted to scream, cry or shoot something. Or all of the above.

A gentle touch on her elbow startled her so badly that she jolted and spun, fists raised.

Ian jerked back, hands up, evidence bag dangling from one. "Whoa. It's just me. And despite what you probably think right now, I come in peace. It's just that peace doesn't always start out that way with him. Never did."

She uncoiled, swallowing past the aching tightness in her throat. "Sorry."

"No. I'm the one who's sorry." He shot a telling look at the door. "I thought from seeing the way he was when he came in, and the way he was with you, that he was... well. I thought he was in a different place, that's all."

"It's not like that." But the heavy weight pressing on her heart said that deep down inside, part of her had hoped.

Not if all he wanted was to be left alone, though. Not if he wanted to be the ranger, the loner, the closed off man who didn't need anything except space and didn't offer anything in return.

He had said he would have his peace and quiet back

in thirteen days, and he hadn't picked the number at random. In thirteen days, the academy assignments were being announced and personnel shifted around. Which meant Tucker had used the information to talk Matt into teaming up with her…and he was looking forward to her departure.

Well, screw him. She could take care of that part right now.

She pulled out her phone, bypassed the first McDermott number and speed-dialed the second.

"McDermott, Homicide."

"It's Gigi. I want to trade in my cop. He's broken."

MATT MADE IT HALFWAY down the hall before he spun and slammed his shoulder into the wall. Pain flared at the point of impact and lower down in his gut, but he deserved all of it and more.

Sagging, he leaned back against the wall, which felt far steadier than he did just now.

One second he and Ian had been doing okay, and then the next…damn it. They'd been back at it like they'd seen each other four days ago, not four years.

And Gigi had been right in the line of fire.

He had caught a glimpse of her face as he stormed out, and the dark-eyed mixture of sharp hurt and dull resignation was singed into his brain. He deserved that, too, because he had insisted that he was the best one to watch her back when really he was about the worst possible choice to protect her.

Which he had just proven in spades.

His emotional control was gone, incinerated the moment their lips touched. Or maybe it had happened before then, somewhere between the first sizzle of seeing her in the hallway outside Tucker's office and the second his brain had kicked back into gear and warned him that she was trouble. That she was the first person he'd met in a very long time who had the potential to mess with his head.

Only she wasn't trying to mess with anything—she was just trying to do her job. He was the mess—what had just happened back there had nothing to do with her and everything to do with old scars, even older dreams, and a friend who knew how to push his buttons.

Damn Ian for going there. Damn Proudfoot for whoring out part of Bear Claw Canyon because he couldn't handle his finances.

And damn him for not being the man he should have been.

Behind him, a door opened and Ian's voice became audible, saying, "...any time, day or night, seriously."

"I may just take you up on that." She sounded as if she really meant it, too, which put a nasty twist in Matt's gut, even though he knew he didn't have the right to feel anything even remotely approaching jealousy right now.

In college, Matt had been the charming jock, Ian the poet, and they'd both had their share of conquests. Later, though, their lives had diverged. Ian had gone to grad school, flourished, and emerged both poet and charmer, while Matt had worked long hours in uniform, trying to make everything okay when it couldn't possibly be. And now Ian was still charming, while Matt was...hell, he didn't know what he was, but it wasn't good.

Ian and Gigi exchanged a few more pleasantries that

had him grinding his teeth, then she headed in his direction, her silver-toed boots clicking like a ticked-off metronome.

She wore a studded black blazer, beige pants that clung to every dip and curve, and a purple shirt that did more than hint at her cleavage. But where yesterday he would have looked at her and seen a city slicker, now he just saw *her*.

He pushed away from the wall as she neared him, stuck his hands in his pockets when they wanted to reach for her. "I know it's not nearly good enough, but I'm sorry. Ian and I…well, he's always been able to get into me like that, just keeps going until I snap."

"He's worried about you."

So am I. It had never been like this for him before, all rage and mood swings, with him feeling like he was barely hanging on. "Give it five minutes and he'll be back to worrying about tracking down those supposed barred eagles. Which is what we should be doing." Not wasting time arguing politics and impossibilities.

She stared at him for a long moment, her hair falling in angles across her face like war paint, making her look in that moment both wholly feminine and terrifyingly capable. "Okay," she said softly. "Let's hit the road."

He had the feeling he had just failed a test he hadn't even known he was taking.

As they rolled away from the U.C. Bear Claw campus, she called the lab, gave a brief report on the eagles, and had Alyssa send a bunch of altitude maps and ore surveys to her phone. When he tapped the brakes at the main road, she broke off her conversation to say, "Head for Station Fourteen. Jack's waiting for me up at your place."

Matt winced at the continued invasion of his private space, but he headed north out of the city without comment. She called someone else, got a different map sent and studied the information on her phone's tiny display, frowning.

He glanced over. "I know you're mad at me—and with good reason—but that's my territory. Talk to me. I can help narrow down the search."

"I'm not mad at you. I'm thinking."

And the thing was, she didn't really look mad. She looked sad and resigned, and the two together tugged at something inside him. "What did Jack find?"

She glanced at him, brows furrowed. "Nothing that I'm aware of. Why?"

"I thought you were going to go over some new— Oh." The detective wasn't waiting to show her evidence. He was picking her up and taking her away.

"You said you wanted your peace and quiet back." She was focused on her maps, or at least staring at them. "You saved my life. Giving you yours back seemed like the least I could do."

"I didn't…" He trailed off as a heavy weight settled on his chest at the realization that she was right that they should split up. Williams had his head on straight. He would do a better job of protecting her, because there wouldn't be any emotion in the mix beyond friendship and respect.

"This is what you want, right?"

For a second the air between them went tight with anticipation; he had a feeling she was waiting for him to argue. When he didn't, she gave a soft sigh and looked out the window.

He told himself to leave it alone, that it was better this way. Instead, after a moment he said, "Have you ever slept wrong on your gun hand, and woke up with it totally numb and useless?"

"I shoot okay lefty." But the corner of her mouth softened a little, and she nodded, still staring out the window as they headed up into the foothills. "Yeah. I know the feeling. And I know how much it hurts when everything starts waking up again, how you just want to stand there and scream, or maybe hit something, because of the pain. But at the same time, you know you have to get through it or you won't be able to shoot properly."

How was it that she could see so clearly something he was just starting to get to himself?

"I thought I put myself back together the best I could. Now, though, I think maybe I've been sleepwalking for the past six years, and this case, meeting you…I'm starting to wake up."

She looked at him then, expression unreadable. "And that back there was what, emotional pins and needles?"

"Whatever it was, it wasn't me. Or not the guy I want to be. Especially not around you."

A flush touched her cheeks, but she looked down and fiddled with her phone. "I'm just passing through. Another thirteen days and I'm out of here, either to the academy or to fill in for someone who's gotten the call."

"Caught that, did you? Yeah, Tucker got word this

morning. I wasn't supposed to say anything until he knew one way or the other. Sorry."

"Don't be. It's a reality. Just like it's a reality that I don't have time for a new complication right now, even a short-term one."

He turned on to the winding route that led alongside brittle, dry Sector Nine to the western half of the back-country. They were alone on the familiar road, so he put the pedal down.

He didn't know whether she had meant to make him think about short-term, no-harm-no-foul sex between them, but he was suddenly filled with her flavor as if he had just kissed her, was warmed by her skin as if he had just touched her. Although his body was on board for short-term anything, logic said she would be far better off riding with Williams. He might be waking back up, but he was far from leveled off.

"Okay," he said quietly. "Yeah. Okay." He glanced up in the rearview mirror to see if he could catch her expression, some glimpse of what she was feeling.

Instead, he saw a truck that hadn't been behind them a minute ago.

It was big and black, with tinted windows. And it was catching up fast.

Chapter Nine

Matt's pulse accelerated and his knuckles went white on the steering wheel. "Hang on," he ordered grimly, "we've got company."

"What?" Gigi craned her head to see out the back just as the rearview mirror caught a flash of metal coming out the passenger's-side window of the vehicle.

"Down!" Matt caught her shirt and dragged her aside a split second before a machine pistol chattered. Cracks spiderwebbed the rear window, radiating from a quartet of bullet holes.

Gigi screamed and flattened herself. More slugs punched through, one whining way too close past Matt's ear.

Cursing, he swerved as much as he dared on the curvy road, trying to stay away from where a guardrail blocked a hell of a drop on their left.

"Call it in!" he snapped. "Tucker first." McDermott wasn't the chief, but he was the one Matt trusted.

Hitting the gas, he sent the Jeep lunging up the steady incline, accelerating away from the heavier truck.

He hugged the high side as much as he dared, blood chilling with the realization that these guys—whoever they were and whatever they wanted—were finished with leaving their victims to die. They were going to make sure they got the job done this time.

Not on my watch, he vowed grimly. And not with Gigi there. If he had been alone he might've tried to turn the tables and get his hands on the bastards chasing him. As it was, all he wanted to do was get the hell out of there, fast.

More bullets came spraying through the back window. Air screamed into the cabin, turning the world to a roar.

When the road straightened out, he concentrated on getting ahead of the truck, out of range.

Gigi was talking into the phone, making her report in a shaky voice. "I don't know," she said, "we're—hang on." She punched her phone to speaker and held it up to him. "Where are we, exactly?"

"West access road, near mile marker ten, in that snaky section with the drop-off."

"Christ," Tucker said. "Okay, cars are on the way, and I'll get a bird in the air. Somehow. Just hang on."

"Planning on it. You're looking for a black truck, late model Dodge half-ton, no front plate."

"On it."

Matt clenched his teeth as he gunned it around a sharp curve going way too freaking fast, and had to hit the brakes. Rubber chirped and the Jeep threatened to tip. But they were still three car lengths or so ahead of the truck.

Gigi braced herself, pocketed her phone, and went for the radio. Her hands were shaking, her eyes stark in her bloodless face, but she was holding it together like a warrior. A cop.

In another lifetime, he would've been proud to have her on his team. In this one, he didn't want her anywhere near the action. He had seen too much, lost too much. But when she racked the radio and pulled her Beretta, he knew the choice was out of his hands. There was no way to keep her out of the action now. He glanced over, met her eyes, and nodded. "Go for the tires on the right." That would send the bastards into the wall, giving him half a chance of getting a witness out of the crash.

They hit a straightaway that flattened and then descended. The truck picked up speed, caught up and the guns came back out.

Gigi found a decent vantage, took aim and fired.

"Headlight," she reported, then cried, "Hang on!"

Matt had seen them coming, but wasn't braced nearly enough for the shuddering impact that ripped through the lighter Jeep when the truck rammed them. He cursed viciously, but the sound was lost beneath the crunch of impact and the scream of tires as the Jeep half-spun and slid sideways, being pushed along by the truck.

That put the two cabs practically on top of each other. Through the heavily tinted windows, he glimpsed the driver's panicked surprise, the passenger's scramble as he tried to clear a jammed clip. The men were strangers, average-looking white guys who were trying to kill him and Gigi.

Acting on fury and instinct, blood going crisis-cold, Matt pulled out his Sig and fired into the tint, aware that Gigi was doing the same with her Beretta. The truck's front windshield cracked and blood splashed inside the cab.

One of them was wounded, but would it be enough?

Then momentum swung the vehicles another ninety degrees, slingshotting the truck ahead of the Jeep just as the road curved. The truck flung free, fishtailing as it headed for the curve.

The Jeep kept sliding sideways, totally at the mercy of momentum.

"Take this!" Matt shoved his gun at Gigi and grabbed the wheel, fighting the top-heavy vehicle when it listed and tried to spin out. A tire blew on the left side, making the drag worse.

The truck's brake lights flashed as the vehicle disappeared around the curve.

But the Jeep wasn't turning fast enough; inertia was dragging it toward the far side of the road, where there was a low guardrail and freefall plunge. Pulse hammering, Matt fought the skid, trying to regain control.

They weren't going to make it.

"Son of a— Hang on!" Giving in, knowing it was the only way, he cut the wheel the other way, hit the brakes, and sent them into a hard spin in the other direction. They whipped around once, twice, then headed for the rock wall.

Letting go of the wheel, he lunged against the restraints of his seat belt and wrapped his arms around Gigi as best he could, shielding her. "Keep your head down!"

They slammed sideways into the wall with a rending *crunch* of metal and a crash from what was left of the glass, the *whumps* of three of the four airbags, and Gigi's soft scream, which was buried in his chest.

His belt burned his hips and shoulder; glass and other fragments pelted him where he was curled around her. But as the Jeep rocked back on its opposite tires and shuddered to crippled stillness, he became aware of a protected strip across the back of his neck and one shoulder, where she had wrapped her free arm around him and spread her hand to cover as much of him as she could reach.

Not daring to name the strange, soft feeling that moved through him, he pulled away from her. But he didn't let go all the way. He couldn't.

As he eased back, her hand slid along the side of his neck and down to flatten on his chest, over his heart, which was beating fast.

Her eyes were wide and dark, her hair an angular slash across her forehead, and the four diamond studs she wore, three and one, twinkled like stars. He realized that all the things that had initially warned him off her had become part of him now, because they were part of what made her uniquely *her*. And somehow, in the space of a day, she had wormed her way inside his heart.

She straightened a little and unwrapped the arm she'd held clutched tightly to her chest between them. In it, she held two guns: his and hers. Which was some seriously quick thinking, because if there was anything worse than spinning a Jeep and slamming it sideways into a big-ass rock, it was doing all that with a couple of pistols bouncing around.

She was a natural.

Any praise he might have given her jammed in his

throat because he didn't know what to say, how to tell her that her instincts and talent impressed him as much as her guts and reckless disregard for her own safety terrified him.

Then they heard the low thump of rotors and the building wail of sirens, and it was too late for him to say anything.

She drew away with a small smile that didn't reach all the way to her eyes, and handed him his Sig. "Nice driving, hotshot. I guess that's two rescues I owe you."

"Let's call it even. Your shooting kept them too busy to take out our tires."

Beyond the drop-off, an unfamiliar stealth-painted chopper suddenly swung up from below the guardrail to hover. It was heavily armed but none of the guns were pointed in their direction, and as Matt watched, the pilot gave them a dip-wiggle that signaled "we're on your side." Where the hell had Tucker dug *that* up?

"Okay. We're even." Without another word, she booted free of the airbag and headed toward the chopper, holstering her gun as she walked…and leaving him kicking himself for missing a moment that suddenly felt like it could have been very important, even if he didn't know what to say.

It's better this way, he told himself. *No complications.* But as he climbed out of the Jeep, his blood was doing a slow burn…not because the bastards in the truck had gotten away from him, but because Gigi was about to.

RIGHT AFTER THE CHOPPER'S arrival, three P.D. vehicles came around the corner and hit the brakes. Within fifteen minutes, Gigi was at the center of a law-enforcement huddle that her competitors for the academy slots would have killed for.

In addition to Tucker, Jack and the seven other Bear Claw cops that had converged on the remote stretch of road, the sleek chopper—whose tail numbers looked suspiciously magnetic—had dropped off Cassie and her husband, FBI analyst Seth Varitek, along with two people Gigi had heard about but never met: Jonah Fairfax and his wife, Chelsea, formerly one of Bear Claw's medical examiners. The two had been instrumental in foiling al-Jihad's terrorist plot, and now worked as partners in an unnamed government agency.

Based on the stories, Gigi had been expecting a pair of glossy superspies like something out of the movies. But while Fairfax—aka Fax—was killer handsome, with ice-blue eyes that instantly seemed to look through her, Chelsea was lovely in a honey-haired, girl-next-door sort of way. The two were clearly very much a part of the Bear Claw gang, fitting seamlessly with Tucker, Cassie and Seth, and razzing Alyssa, who was attending the meeting by speakerphone and was trying not to be too cranky about being left out.

In contrast, Matt stood well apart from the group near the guardrail, staring into the abyss.

A couple of times Gigi started to call him over, but stopped herself. He was a grown-up; he could join or not, his choice.

Besides, even though for a second there she had thought that he might finally be seeing her for who and what she really was, the evidence said otherwise. He was in a weird headspace right now, and if he needed to get away from the crowd, it was the least she could do for him. She owed him her life. Again.

He might think they were even, but she knew better. And a Lynd always paid her debts. So she bought him the room he seemed to need by briefing the others on the attack and describing—as best she could, anyway— the truck and its occupants, who seemed to have disappeared into thin air.

"They're down a headlight and windshield," she finished, "and the driver took at least one bullet." She was pleased that her voice sounded level and businesslike. That was no small feat given that she was holding on to her cool by force of will, along with the inner promise that she could have the shakes later, in private, for as long as she needed to.

"Was either of them the guy who knocked you down during the fire?" Jack asked.

She thought about it, tried to picture it, but shook her head. "I barely saw him." The whole shoot-out was a blur of fear and the ping-whine of ricochets. And she didn't want to admit it, but Matt had been right—shooting was different when the cardboard cutout wasn't cardboard, and it was shooting back.

"I'll check the hospitals for any gunshot victims coming in over the next few hours," Alyssa said from the speakerphone, "then see what I can do on the truck."

"Seth and I can process the Jeep and the rest of the scene," Cassie said, eyeing the crumpled vehicle and the trail of tire marks and glass that stretched around the far turn. "That should keep us busy for a while."

Gigi's body sang with bruises that hadn't yet formed. She couldn't believe it was barely noon, but she manned up. "I'll help."

"The hell you will," Tucker said mildly, though there

was steel in his eyes. "You're out of here until tomorrow morning at the earliest. Both of you."

"But—"

"Take some downtime. We'll call you if something breaks."

She drew breath to argue, then realized she didn't want to. Letting out a long sigh, she nodded. "Okay, yeah. Thanks." Glancing at the Jeep, she said, "I think I'm going to need a ride back to the city, though."

Tucker and Jack both started to protest, but Matt's voice overrode them. "Not the city." He pushed through the crowd and stopped facing her, ignoring the others. "And not alone. Those guys came after us specifically… and they were shooting to kill. Not all that well, which, along with the expression on the driver's face when he got a close-up of my pistol, tells me they're not pros. But that doesn't make them any less dangerous. They missed, and one of them is hurt, but if we're right about there being a bunch of them, those two will be calling in reinforcements."

"They… Right." Gigi pressed a hand to her stomach as it went suddenly raw. "Of course, you're right." He was standing way too close, his strength making her want to lean, despite everything.

"The break room at the lab should be safe," Cassie suggested.

"We can do better than that," Chelsea said. She glanced at Fax, got a nod of assent. "We've got a little place outside the city, part getaway spot, part safe house. It's tight as a tick, so if you want, you can lock yourself in and forget about the world without needing any additional manpower." She crouched for a second, fiddled with what looked like a high-tech ankle holster and came up with a keyless fob, which she held out.

"That sounds like heaven," Gigi said fervently. "I'm in."

"*We're* in," Matt corrected, and snagged the fob.

Something sparked deep inside her, feeling suddenly very different from the near-tears of moments earlier. She wanted it to be irritation. "I'm riding with Jack from now on, remember?"

He cursed under his breath. "Fine. Then he stays in the safe house, too. I don't want you going it alone."

She drew breath to snarl, then stopped when her mind played back Ian's parting words to her: *Blackie's coming back from a really dark place. I'd rather he didn't have to go it alone.*

She hadn't been able to give Ian the reassurance he'd been looking for. Now, though, empathy tugged when she saw echoes of her own fatigue and stress in Matt's expression. He acted as if she shouldn't trust him, but then he'd been there each and every time she'd needed him.

He hadn't asked her to give him a chance…but Ian had. And, oddly, she trusted the ornithologist when she wasn't sure she trusted herself anymore.

So, finally, she nodded. "It makes more sense for the two of us to stay together than for me to tie up Jack's time." She needed to take a break someplace safe…and maybe she didn't want to go it alone after all.

THE SMALL LOG CABIN, which was ninety minutes or so on the other side of the city from the crash, was made of some sort of impenetrable composite and boasted a

warren of tunnels that led to concealed doorways sprin-
kled across the ten-acre property, several of which were
outfitted with go bags and getaway vehicles.

As Matt rolled the rented Blazer into the attached
garage, and blast doors glided into place behind the vehicle, he noted three different levels of security, figured
he had probably missed several others and decided he
felt good about the setup.

He wasn't so sanguine about the situation, though.
The part of him that needed to be there with Gigi, to
know she was safe and taking care of herself, was offset
by the part of him that said it was a really bad idea
for the two of them to spend the night under the same
roof.

Then again, safe houses weren't exactly known for
their ambience. The handful he'd been in over the years
had all been boxy and practical, with enough bedrooms
for the protectee and several marshals or cops. He should
be able to stay close, yet keep his distance.

"You coming in or staying out here?" she asked.
She stood at an inner door that led from the garage to
the main cabin, holding the keyless fob, one eyebrow
raised.

"Coming in." He joined her as she used the fob and
a security code to open the reinforced door, and they
stepped through together.

And stopped dead. Because this was no safe house.
It was a freaking armor-plated love nest.

Chapter Ten

Gigi swallowed hard. "Um. This is…cozy."

What had looked like a modest two stories from the outside proved to be a single main room with a vaulted cathedral ceiling, decorated in warm neutrals with splashes of local art. A small kitchen took up one of the short walls and a huge fieldstone fireplace spanned the other.

But her attention was fixed on the wide stone-veneered platform that began at the hearth, took up half of the main room…and housed a sunken hot tub approximately the size of her apartment's bedroom. There were multiple connected pools, some deep and jetted, others shallow and smooth. And some were just the size of two bodies intertwined.

Bolsters were scattered around, bright colors against the composite surface. And there was a console that would have done the Enterprise proud controlling the tub and fireplace, along with an entertainment center she suspected was also jacked into the security cameras.

The other half of the main room offered a sunken living room furnished with a wide, plush couch that was practically a bed itself, and a thick, plush carpet strewn with pillows. There were two doors on the long wall, one leading to a bathroom, the other a bedroom.

The hot tub was dry and drained; a discreet placard on the wall described the eco-friendly solar heating, scrubbing and recycling protocols, and listed the number of the maid service that had been cleared onto the property. A panel beside the door they had come through offered a second security hub along with a touch screen computer that, once they used the log-in sequences Fax had given them, would provide full data access as well as information on the cabin's defenses and escape routes.

But those stark practicalities did nothing to lessen the sudden suggestive intimacy of the space.

"What," Matt said drily, "no bearskin rug?"

Her face heated. "I'm sure they figured that would be over the top."

"Like this isn't?" But he notched the go bag he'd rescued from the wrecked Jeep a little higher on one shoulder. "You want the first shower?"

For a moment, she just stared at the tub and felt every bone in her body ache. Then she nodded and headed for the bathroom, allowing herself a harmless tug of envy for Chelsea, who had not only found herself an über-spy, she held her own against him. They worked together, functioned together as a team. And, apparently, enjoyed their getaway time.

Gigi didn't let herself look back at Matt, didn't let herself wish for things that weren't going to happen. Instead, she went into the bathroom, closed the door, turned the luxurious shower to its highest settings, stripped down and climbed in. Then she curled herself into a ball in the corner, pressed her face into her knees and waited for the storm.

It didn't come.

Always before, in the aftermath of terror had come the tears, the emotional outpouring that had, oddly, made her feel normal, as if it said "yes, you're a woman, not a robot." She wasn't fearless, wasn't nearly as brave as others thought her. But she was good at setting the doubts aside for a few hours, even days, and just dealing.

At the age of eleven, she had spent three days alone, lost on the Appalachian Trail when a freak storm had separated her from the rest of her family. She had dealt, she had survived and she had eventually found her way back to the main trail. And she hadn't shed a single tear until she saw her parents and sisters rushing toward her—at which point she had sat down in the dirt and howled.

It had been like that ever since: she subsumed the fear and did what needed to be done, then weathered the weepy aftermath.

Only now there weren't any tears. There was only a hollow, tired ache and the sense that this was the first of the many chases, many adrenaline rushes that would come with being on a crisis response team.

Which was what she wanted.

Right?

But just as she couldn't summon the emotional release that usually helped her clear her head after she made it through a dangerous situation, she didn't have an immediate answer to that question.

She tried to tell herself she was tired, strung out and

pent up. Only she didn't feel all that tired, and she didn't feel like crying. Instead, she felt alive and alert, and intensely aware of her surroundings. The water was warm, the tiles cool, slick and not very comfortable.

Finally giving up on the idea of a good crying jag— maybe she just couldn't let down her guard all the way knowing Matt was out in the other room—she dragged herself upright and finished showering, feeling restless and dissatisfied.

Too late, she remembered Chelsea's offer of spare clothes in the bedroom. But there were clean robes folded on a rack, and she couldn't face putting back on an outfit that stank of fear. Hesitating only briefly, she pulled on one of the robes, belted it firmly, and headed out into the main room, expecting to step from the shower's fog into cool, dry air.

She got warm humidity instead, along with the smell of grilled cheese from the kitchen. She stalled at the sight of the filled hot tub under turned-low lights and the flickering illumination of a small fire that provided more ambience than warmth. Motor noise hummed a soothing monotone, jets and bubbles did their thing, frothing the surface of the water, and a Bose radio was tuned to something low and jazzy. There was no sign of Matt, and the bedroom door was closed.

He had set the scene for luxurious pleasure…and then shut himself away.

The message was clear: *You've got your space, I've got mine.*

Instead of turning her off or making her angry, it made the gesture that much more poignant. It made her feel cared for, tended to. And it made her ache for him.

She let out a soft sigh. "He's right. It's better this way."

She was already in danger of falling hard for the complications and losing sight of what mattered. And he was in a weird place, not yet sure if he wanted to be his old self, some new incarnation, or the loner who disappeared into the backcountry, shutting out the people who wanted to care about him.

Yeah, the closed door was the right call. But as she headed for the kitchen and found the plate he had fixed for her, along with a cooling cup of herbal tea, she caught herself eyeing the door, wondering if it was locked. And wondering, too, what would happen if she knocked.

Don't go there.

She didn't let herself stand near the door and listen, picturing him on the other side doing the same thing. Instead, she took her meal up to the hot tub, debating only briefly before she slipped off her robe and climbed in. The warmth surrounded her instantly with cheerful bubbles that burst against her skin, easing the sting of the day.

She lay back, closed her eyes and thought about the fading ache of bruises, the noise the crash had made, and the way he had hung on to her at the last minute and shielded her with his body.

She thought about her condo back in Denver, and how it would feel to be there alone after a day like today.

She pictured Chelsea and Fax winging through the air in the sleek black helicopter, laughing as they agreed that yes, a bearskin rug would definitely be too much for the safe house.

She heard the soft cadence of Alyssa's voice as she

and Tucker did the "Hello, McDermott, Forensics, this is McDermott, Homicide," thing.

And, finally knowing what she needed to do, she reached for the phone handset that rested near the hot tub's controls, and used the secure landline to dial out.

When the call went live, she took a deep breath and said, "Mom? It's Gigi. I need a reality check."

MATT PACED THE BIG bedroom like a cougar behind a chain-link fence: restless, edgy and angry. It was tempting to pretend the frustration came entirely from him wanting to be out there working the case, but he knew damn well that if he was out there he would've been wishing himself right back inside the safe house.

He wanted to be there with her, for her, wanted to watch over her, protect her. But that was the lie cops told themselves, that it was possible for one human being to ensure the safety of another. It was a comforting illusion, one that gave them purpose and kept them going when knives flashed and bullets flew. But it was just an illusion.

Accidents happened. Crimes happened. People died because they were in the wrong place at the wrong time.

Aware that he had his Sig in his hand and was methodically dropping the clip and slapping it home, over and over again in a jittery tic he had conquered by his second month on the job, he set the weapon aside and reached for the phone. Line one was lit, so he punched the second line and went through the motions of getting himself patched into the radio up at his house, resigned to the fact that someone would be there.

Sure enough, there was an answer right away. "Station Fourteen."

So much had happened over the past few days that it took him a few seconds to place the voice. "Jim?"

"Hey, boss." Anticipating the question, the younger ranger said, "No, she's not awake yet. But she's stable, and her parents flew in, so I figured I'd come back up and put in some hours."

Hearing fatigue in the other man's voice, Matt said, "I hope some of those hours are bunk time. Or I guess couch time."

"I can sleep later, once we've got these bastards," Jim said, voice low and fervent. He didn't really sound like a kid anymore.

"Yeah. I know how you feel. What's the latest?"

"Nothing and more nothing." The answer was laden with disgust. "There's no sign of her Jeep anywhere in Sector Fourteen—at least as far as we can tell with the really sketchy air-search time Bert has managed to beg, borrow and steal."

"Her attackers must've driven it out."

"Or stuck it in a cave. Either way, it doesn't look like that's going to lead us anywhere."

"How about focusing on places you might expect to see a barred eagle?"

"Your bird guy says we're looking at only two places in Sector Fourteen—we're pretty low on copper ore—and a few more in Twelve and Thirteen. Bert is checking them out."

"Alone?"

"Hell, no. The place is crawling with volunteers. The parking lot has gone tent city."

Oddly, the thought brought only dull surprise—and gratitude—at the way the ranger crews had banded together and volunteered their time. "Make sure nobody goes off alone."

"Yeah." Jim hesitated. "Is this about Tanya's old boyfriend, do you think?"

Matt's attention sharpened away from the window, where he'd been blindly staring out at the treeline as the late afternoon edged toward dusk. "Maybe. Why? What do you know about him?"

"She told me how he died in that jailbreak a couple of years ago. She never said it in so many words, but it seemed to me that she felt like it was her fault, because he wouldn't have been in Bear Claw if it weren't for her. I guess he asked her to stay with him back east, even get married, but she wanted to keep skiing and wasn't sure about the marriage thing, so she came here instead. A couple of months later, he got a job in the ME's office and followed her. I think she figures that if she hadn't wanted to ski so badly, they both would've stayed back east and he wouldn't have died." He paused, then added, "At least not that way."

Definitely not a kid anymore.

"The cops aren't sure whether or not the murder is connected to what's going on right now," Matt said, "but regardless, I want you watching your back, okay?" And even though he was out of the business of managing other people's lives, he added, "Don't feel like you have to stay up there, either. It sounds like Bert's got plenty of help, so you should take all the time you want down at the hospital."

"Count on it. I'm planning on being the first thing she sees when she wakes back up. I want her to know how I feel about her right away, and that I'll be there for her, no matter what."

"Okay." A heavy weight pressed on Matt's chest. "Good. That's good."

"I spent too much time waiting for her to get over the ex and making sure I knew what I was feeling, and… well. I'm not going to make that mistake again. Just because the timing isn't perfect doesn't change the way we feel about each other."

Matt tried to tell himself that wouldn't sound nearly so profound if he weren't closed in an armored bedroom, elementally aware of the woman on the other side of the door, and the fact that they felt something for each other despite being at completely different places in their lives.

He cleared his throat. "Okay, kid. Stay safe. And tell Tanya's family that we're all pulling for her."

"Will do." Jim signed off and the airwaves went blank, hissing with static. But that was nothing compared to the thoughts buzzing in Matt's mind as he stood alone in the bedroom, barefoot and wearing the worn black cargo pants and plain white T-shirt he kept in his go bag.

He didn't feel like the ranger, or even the cop. It was like those other pieces of him had been temporarily emptied out so he could be someone else for a few hours—maybe even the man he would have become if things had been different.

But that man also knew he was coming down off an adrenaline high and working on zero sleep. And he couldn't tell if that was making things more or less clear.

He wanted Gigi like he wanted his next breath, and he knew that the chemistry went both ways, but the timing was just plain wrong. Her life was poised to explode in new, exciting directions. His life was…well, he didn't know anymore what it was doing, or where he wanted it to go next, and that was a large part of the problem.

She was burning up the pavement while he'd been standing still. Even if he got moving now, he wouldn't be able to catch up and might not be going in the same direction. They might collide, but he didn't see how they could get in step together.

Was there a workable solution? Damned if he knew. But one thing was certain: he wasn't going to last much longer in that bedroom. She was too close, his memories of the chase too fresh. He could be sitting looking down at her lying in a hospital bed like Tanya. Or worse, a casket.

But they had survived unscathed and for now, at least, they were safe.

More, Jim's words about not wanting to wait too long kept colliding with the pins-and-needles sensation that had been chasing Matt ever since he kissed Gigi, the two together letting him know that sometimes it wasn't possible to wait for the perfect moment, the perfect plan. Hell, he didn't have a plan, didn't know what he was expecting. All he knew was that he couldn't sit in that bedroom alone another minute if there was any chance she was feeling half of what he was.

Already moving before he was consciously aware of having made the decision, he crossed to the door. He cracked it and heard her voice, opened it all the way and saw her reclining in the hot tub, mostly submerged in bubbles, with her wet hair slicked back from her face, her eyes closed, and her head tipped back against the curving wall of the faux stone surround.

With the fire in the background, candles around the edges and music carrying just over the water's burble, the space was a warm, comforting fantasy that put him instantly on edge and told him this wasn't a good idea, that it was as much an illusion as his peace and quiet had turned out to be.

He took a big step back and reached for the door. But then he hesitated, empathy tugging when he realized that Gigi might be surrounded by soft luxury, but she didn't look comforted. She looked stark.

A woman's voice emerged from a hidden speaker. "We're keeping our fingers crossed for you, baby. Call us the minute you hear anything, okay?"

"I will," she said softly. "'Bye, Mom. I love you."

"We love you, too, sweetie."

Those simple, profound words cut through him and left him aching for the things he'd lost. But at the same time, there was a dullness in Gigi's voice, a sense that she was deeply disappointed.

The line went dead, but it was a long moment before she sighed and stirred, reaching across to cut the call.

"She doesn't know what's happening out here, does she?" he asked.

She stiffened, but didn't do the jerk-gasp-squeak routine he would have expected from so many other women.

Instead, she slowly opened her eyes. "How long have you been standing there?"

He suspected that she meant to glare, but the effect was ruined by an air of quiet unhappiness. It tugged at him, drew him closer, until he was standing at the edge of the hot-tub platform. He was all too aware that her robe was draped nearby, her skin pink beneath the swirling, bubbling water. "Just through the goodbyes. Did you tell her about the fire and the crash?"

For a second he didn't think she was going to answer. Then she looked away and sank a little deeper, so the water covered her shoulders. "I was going to—that's why I called her. I was going to tell her everything, ask her what she thought about…well, all of it. But then she started asking about the academy, all excited for me, and I just couldn't. It's taken this long for her to stop asking 'are you okay?' right off the bat every time I call. I just…"

She shrugged, the movement causing ripples in the restless water. "She doesn't need to worry about me. I can take care of myself." She paused, lips quirking. "And now you're going to tell me that someone sure as hell needs to worry about my reckless butt, and how I don't take care of myself nearly as well as I'd like to think."

He might have, but he was caught up in the sudden realization that even though she was surrounded by friends and intimately connected to her family, at the same time she was, in her own way, very isolated.

Maybe because of that realization, or the strange emptiness inside him and the things Jim had been saying about the dangers of waiting too long, he found that it wasn't all that hard for him to say what he'd been meaning to say. "You know how I said I would tell you later why I left L.A.?"

She nodded slowly, eyes sharpening on him.

"Well, it's later." He paused. "That is, if you still want to hear the story."

Her lips parted in surprise. She hesitated, and for a second he thought she was going to be the smarter, saner one by turning him down. But then she reached over to dial up more bubbles, obscuring his glimpses of pink skin beneath the water, and patted the soft faux stone beside her.

"Come and put your feet in, at least," she said softly. "The water helps."

And so, he realized, did the feeling of moving toward something for a change, rather than walking away.

Chapter Eleven

Gigi made herself keep breathing as he levered himself easily up onto the platform and padded toward her, barefoot. His faded black pants had slipped below his hipbones and his white T-shirt clung, dampening in the humid air.

With any of the fun, insubstantial men she had spent time with over the years, she would have stripped those last few pieces of clothing off him and pulled him, laughing, into the hot tub with her. More, a small, panicked part of her brain said that would be safer than peeling back this layer. Not because she feared she wouldn't like the man beneath, but because she was badly afraid she would, and she wasn't sure she could afford it.

That scared part of her said to run. Instead, she stayed put as he rolled up his pants to reveal masculine, muscular calves and the hint of a small surgical scar below one knee.

His eyes followed hers and a corner of his mouth kicked up. "I tore my ACL trying to get around this tall, obnoxious guy during a pickup basketball game my freshman year of college. Ian busted me up back then, and he's been doing it ever since."

It was the kind of small detail she had never cared about with other men. Now she stored the information away as he sat beside her, let his feet drop into the water, and braced himself on his palms.

His entry sent new currents brushing along her body, touching her breasts and thighs. Not that she needed anything to heighten the churning burn of desire. It had taken root the moment she saw him in the bedroom doorway, eyes dark with an emotion she couldn't name. Didn't dare.

Okay, this so wasn't going to work. "Close your eyes," she ordered. "And no peeking."

When she was pretty sure he had obeyed, she grabbed the robe and climbed out of the hot tub, wrapping the garment around her.

Then, feeling better armored with a layer of white terry cloth around her rather than bubbles, she sat beside him, slipped her feet into the water beside his, and said, "Okay. Start talking."

He didn't say anything at first, which made her think the moment had come and gone.

But then, without looking at her, he said, "The summer before my senior year in college, my father's chopper went down during a National Guard training exercise. When my mother heard that he was being rushed to a trauma center about an hour away, she and my fifteen-year-old sister Lena jumped in the car and took off." His voice was almost inflectionless, as though time or repetition had robbed the story of its emotion. "They ran a red light a couple of miles from home and got T-boned by a furniture truck. They both died instantly."

Oh, she thought. *Oh, no.* A soft sound escaped her.

She had heard the stories the cops told at Shakey's after shift—about families devastated by multiple blows at once, wretched coincidences where even the survivors were victims. But she couldn't imagine—didn't *want* to imagine—the pain.

He continued: "Ian and I were in France, spending a month before school started back up. It took the authorities two days to track us down, took me another day and a half to get home. They had been dead four days before I made it back."

Gigi nearly closed her eyes to block out his pain. But then, knowing that was the coward's way out, she instead reached out to him. He didn't offer a hand, didn't offer anything, just stayed braced back on his palms, staring into the bubbling water. She wrapped her fingers around his wrist and squeezed, feeling his pulse beneath her fingers. "I'm sorry."

"It was a long time ago."

"Not for you."

"Yeah." He unbent a little, shifted and took her hand. He twined his fingers through hers so gently that tears prickled behind her eyes, though she didn't let him see.

"Afterward, the whole political science thing seemed…pointless, like it was just people sitting around and arguing about stuff most of them would never need to worry about. I wanted to make an immediate difference in peoples' lives, make things safer for them, better."

"So you became a cop."

He paused, mouth twisting in a humorless smile. "I lost my father because of a freak mechanical problem, my mother and sister because of distracted driving and bad timing, not any sort of crime. But yeah. I became a cop. Within a few years I was the guy they called on for the tricky stuff, the one who always went in the door first. I was promoted to SWAT, then to team leader. For nearly three years, Team Four cleared more tricky situations without casualties than any other team…and then the odds caught up with us."

He let go of her hand and scrubbed at his face, then dropped his arm and just sat there, wrists dangling between his knees. "It was a hostage call, which always adds to the pucker factor because you've got civilians in there, and it was at a bank, which sucks for the obvious reasons. The robbers weren't pros, which meant they were twitchy on the triggers, and…" He shook his head. "My team wasn't in great shape—one guy's wife had just walked out on him, another guy had just found out he had a second kid on the way. They said they were good to go, that they could put that stuff aside… Hell, I don't know. I know prescience isn't part of the job description, but afterward, looking back, I could see the signs."

"I'm sorry," she said again, because it was the truth. What else was there to say?

She had guessed it had been a crisis response gone wrong, but she ached doubly for him now.

"We were in position, waiting on the hostage negotiator and a few feds who were en route, when the shooting started. Later, we found out that a construction worker had gotten it in his head to play hero and went after one of the thieves. All I knew was that we couldn't wait. We breached and went in on the intel we had at hand, which was good but not great. We thought there were four gunmen. Turns out there were five, and the fifth guy knew where to aim, how to go in over and under the body armor, and through the joints."

Thus the scars high and low on his torso. Gigi's stomach did a slow roll. "How many casualties?"

His eyes had gone dead and his voice was flat with pain. "They took out twelve hostages before we breached. Three more were wounded in the crossfire, their bullets, not ours. We got all five of them within, what? Two minutes? Three? But I lost four good officers, including the two guys who had other things on their minds."

"Other things," she echoed. "Like people they cared about."

He didn't seem to hear her. Or maybe he did and didn't know what to say. He continued: "I took a couple of bullets, lost a chunk of my liver and gained an ulcer. And after I finished rehab, I…I don't know. Tuned out, I guess, or maybe burned out. I passed the psych evaluation, but I just couldn't do it anymore. I couldn't go into a call knowing I was putting my teammates' lives on the line, and that us going in there—wherever 'there' was—could upset the balance and start the shooting again. I lasted three months with SWAT, another three in plainclothes before I quit, moved out here, found some peace and quiet, and thought I had healed just fine." He glanced at her, expression as fierce and unreadable as it had been the first time they met. "And then you showed up, and the pins and needles started."

She took his arm in both of hers, leaned against him and pressed her cheek to his T-shirt-clad shoulder, over the bullet scar. "No matter what happens next, I'm glad we got to know each other."

In such a short amount of time, he had become more important to her than she wanted to admit. He annoyed her, intrigued her, turned her on, made her look at things differently. He hadn't quit because he wasn't good enough; he had flamed out because he'd cared too much, put too much of himself into the job. She was happy that he was starting to reconnect with the people and things that had once been important to him.

And when she left… No. She didn't want to think about that right now. Tonight was tonight.

"That's the question, isn't it?" he said quietly. "What, exactly, *does* happen next?" He paused. "Just now, Jim was talking about sitting with Tanya and regretting the things he hadn't done because the timing didn't feel right. And I can't help thinking that either of us could've wound up in the same position today."

She shifted to face him as her heart thudded quickly. Although that small, cautious kernel of self-preservation inside her said to keep her distance, the larger part of her wanted to lean in.

Maybe it was the soft light and the bubbling backdrop, or maybe it was having spent some serious time thinking about death and dying, but the whole idea of avoiding the big foam finger of emotion didn't seem nearly as critical as it had a few days earlier.

Still she didn't want to let him know how huge those emotions were, how all-consuming. He was having enough trouble managing his own head, he shouldn't have to deal with hers, as well.

So she let him see she was serious, didn't let him see her yearn. "I've always said I'd rather have regrets about the things I did do, rather than the things I didn't."

"Why am I not surprised?" For a second, the super-cop was back in his expression, as if he wanted to warn her to be careful, stay back, duck and cover.

His sudden fierceness didn't irritate her as it would have before, because now she knew where he was coming from. More, seeing him in full-on cop mode set off a chain reaction of heat inside her, because for all that she wanted to be the best at what she did, it got her seriously hot when she met someone who was better.

Mixed in with the heat was tenderness, though, because beneath that capability was the weight of responsibility.

"Hey," she said softly, cupping his face in her hands and feeling the bristle of afternoon growth. "We're safe, remember? You can let yourself be off duty for a few hours."

He lifted his hands and caught her wrists, handcuffing her in place. "That's the problem. I can't compartmentalize anymore—hell, I wasn't ever very good at it. I just sucked up the stuff that bothered me. Now, though, I can't separate this case from the thing that's bothering me the most."

"And what is that?" she asked, even though she already knew. It was in the intensity of his eyes and the hard, unyielding grip that said he wasn't going to let her go this time, wasn't going to push her away.

"You," he rasped. The word both thrilled and intimidated her, making the moment feel far more important than it should, far more than she was comfortable with.

She had thought she was out of her comfort zone before, but she hadn't known the half of it.

She was outside the box, outside her usual paradigm, and she didn't care.

The firelight and candles painted him bronze and the humidity had made his hair curl at the tips, contrasting with the hard angles and intensity of his face. His damp T-shirt clung to the bulges of his shoulders and biceps, the ripples of his abs, and his pants were worn enough to drape suggestively, drawing her eyes to the flat planes of his hips and the strong columns of his thighs.

But it was that small nick of a scar below his knee that caught her attention. It was nothing compared to his bullet scars, but it was part of the history he had drifted away from. It gave him a past, marked a time in his life when he still had his parents and sister, still had dreams of going into politics. Those things were gone, but the guy who'd given him the injury wasn't. Anyone who had kept an Ian in his life all this time wasn't nearly the loner he wanted to think.

And, loner or not, cop or ranger, she wanted him. Now. Tonight.

As if her body had been waiting for that permission, heat flooded her, pooling in her breasts and core, and making her very aware that she was naked beneath the robe, that only a thin tie separated them.

His voice rasped low as he said, "I watch you, worry about you, think about you when I should be concentrating on other things." He paused, expression shifting. "Look, I know you've got other plans, and that you don't want to start something with someone as screwed up as me...so here's your chance. Say the word and I'll hole up in the bedroom until morning."

"And my other option?" Her heart tapped a quick rhythm in her chest. *Tonight is tonight,* she thought. She could do this. She could enjoy him yet protect a piece of herself.

"You're the overachiever. You figure it out."

Lips curving, she shifted her hands in his grip and moved in, conscious of the way her robe gaped at the chest as she rose up onto her knees to lean over him. Catching one of his hands, she brought it to the bend of her knee and up along her bare thigh, then pressed her hand atop his, holding him there.

His eyes fired and his fingers flexed restlessly beneath hers as he waited for her kiss. "Just do it," he rasped.

"That's a family motto," she whispered bare inches from his lips.

Then she looped her free hand around his neck and flung herself backward, yanking him fully clothed into the bubbling froth, laughing. Feeling free.

MATT SURFACED WITH A shout and found himself standing nearly chest-deep. He hauled her into his arms as warm, foamy water ran down them both. "You're insane. You know that, right?"

She latched her legs around his waist, flung her arms wide and leaned back into the bubbles. "Sanity is overrated, especially at a time like this."

She had a point—they were in an oasis of calm in the middle of a crisis, and she was in his arms. If this was crazy, maybe he *was* overrating sanity. But there was no way to overrate her wet, gleaming skin.

The robe clung to her breasts but parted between and below, flaring away beneath the bubbles, so when his hands came up naturally to catch her legs where they wrapped around him, his fingers slid without interruption along sleek skin covering gloriously toned muscle.

Murmuring approval, she slicked her hair away from her face and rose back up against him, wrapping her arms around his neck to meet him in an openmouthed, rapacious kiss.

Heat hammered through him, around him. His shaft hardened to iron as it had been that morning when he woke thinking of her.

They kissed, straining together in a clash of lips and tongues that nearly sent him over the edge then and there.

His fingers tightened on her thighs, digging in as he searched for control. He wanted to drag off his pants and bury himself in her, wanted to rise over her, pin her to the tub's edge and pound into her, claiming her as his own.

Slow down. Hold it together. He said it over and over again in his head, clawing himself back from the brink as he held her, kissed her, touched that glorious skin where it slipped and slid against him.

Her robe came loose. His free hand found a breast, and she arched into him. He cupped her for a moment, relearning the feel of a woman's body, learning the feel that was hers alone. Then he slid his thumb up and across, and caught her moan in his mouth as he brushed across a peaked nipple. He kissed her cheek, her jaw, took her earlobe in his mouth and got a raw kick of pleasure from her throaty gasp and the texture of the three diamond studs that were so elementally *Gigi*.

She reared back and peeled his shirt away. His balance teetered in slow motion, the two of them buoyed by the pulsing water that now touched his bare torso.

He let momentum carry them into the shallows, then sat where a curve in the hot tub wall formed a soft niche. It was just right for a man to sit, for a woman to ride. She straddled him, bore him back against the edge, and rose over him as they kissed.

She was naked now, her robe lost somewhere to the water, freeing him to shape the flow of her spine, the flare of her waist and the tight curves of her rear.

His head spun. His body pulsed. For the first time in an eternity, he was entirely inside his own skin and in the moment. He wasn't thinking or worrying, wasn't numb. He was *feeling*. He felt the scrape of her teeth along his throat, the press of her lips on the puckered scar atop his shoulder, bringing mingled arousal and absolution.

Then she straightened and, with an impish smile, disappeared beneath the bubbles. "Don't—" he began, then groaned at the brush of her hair against his stomach, the touch of her lips along the second, larger scar, and the sensation of her fingers at the button of his fly, and then inside.

He hissed and arched into her touch, his vision graying as her hand closed around him fleetingly, then released so she could work his pants off.

As the clinging cloth finally came free, leaving him

naked in the bubbles, she surfaced with a gasp, her eyes bright, her cheeks flushed. He reached for her and she slid up against him, so they half reclined, touching along the lengths of their bodies with her legs alongside his, her arms around his waist, the two of them locked in a kiss.

Then she rose up over him, poised above him. They traded whispered words about safety and protection, and dealt with the necessities. But his entire attention was on need and sensation, the touch of skin on skin, and the way his flesh surged up toward her opening, seeking her. He surged against her, started to shift them and reverse their positions, but she pressed his shoulders back, her lips curving in an expression that was so wholly feminine it made his chest ache.

She leaned in and whispered close to his ear, "How about you let someone take care of you for a change?"

Then she shifted down and back, and he hissed out a breath as his hard tip nudged against yielding flesh and eased inside.

"Ah," he breathed, the noise rattling in his chest. "Tight."

She murmured something against his throat, then found his lips with hers, letting him control the kiss as she controlled their union. She slid down on him inch by torturous inch, until she was finally seated against him, wringing a deep groan from him that felt like it came from his toes.

His whole body stung with pins and needles now, reawakening to pleasure at a level he had never known. His hands flexed on her hips, drawing her closer, settling her astride him until she gasped against his mouth, shuddering as he hit a spot that was sweet, tight and right.

Her inner muscles pulsed around him, waking every neuron and tickling pleasure centers he had long forgotten. Then she began to move, in just a small, wavelike motion at first, following the rhythm of the water surrounding them. Even those small shifts had him throwing back his head and bracing, trying to slow himself down.

Some part of him said that he should be doing the work and making sure she came before he did, but then she picked up the pace, and chivalry lost out to "oh, hell, yeah" as everything started coming together inside him.

Water splashed between them, around them. He let go of her hips and slapped for purchase, found handholds and dug in with his heels, which gave them an anchor but left him effectively bound spread-eagled in the water.

Heat flared where she twined around him, moved against him. He sought her mouth, felt her shudder and clutch as they hit that sweet spot together, and then, too quickly, the pins and needles were racing through him, coalescing, speeding up, threatening to detonate.

He reared up and caught her by the waist, bracing her against the side of the tub as he plunged into her once, twice, a third time, and heard her cry out as he cut loose. Bowing into her, he rode out the orgasm, emptying himself into her in a rush that blew his mind and shifted something deep inside him.

He shuddered against her, pulsed into her, and then held her close as things leveled off and the intensity of their union eased. He kissed her cheek, her temple, wanting to say something, but unable to come up with the right words. Restless, edgy energy shifted inside him; he wasn't even close to sated.

The room suddenly seemed very quiet, with only the hum of machinery, the pop of bubbles and the soft throb of jazz in the background.

It had been a long time since someone had wanted to be there for him, even temporarily, rather than the reverse. She cared for him, made him feel alive again, and he should be satisfied with that. But he found that he couldn't uncoil, couldn't relax, because deep down inside, he knew he hadn't gotten all of her just then. In controlling their lovemaking, she had held part of herself in check.

Don't complicate things, he told himself. *She doesn't want more than this.* He wasn't sure he did, either. But the edge remained.

She curled against him, her head in the crook of his neck, her arms linked loosely around him, their legs tangling as they drifted into deeper water.

"Nice," she said, turning her face into his throat. "Never would've guessed you were rusty."

That elicited a surprised snort out of him. And it gave him an opening to take what he wanted in a way she could understand.

"That's it," he growled. "Those are fighting words." In a rush, he shifted her, got her over his shoulder and charged out of the hot tub, headed for the bedroom.

She squeaked and squirmed wetly. "What are you doing?"

"Getting us someplace drier where I can do this my way."

"You're *complaining?*"

"Hell, no. But you got to go first. Now it's my turn." And this time he would take more. He wanted her to be right there with him in the crazy, illogical space they made together, the sizzle and spark that had forced him out of his comfortable routine and opened old wounds. After tonight, he didn't want to look back and know they had taken it only partway.

Tonight he wanted all of her. No regrets.

Chapter Twelve

Somewhere in the back of Gigi's mind a warning pinged, saying that this was a bad idea, that they should keep it in the hot tub, on the couch, the bolsters, hell, up against the wall. Those were places where sex stayed fun, where they were just two people burning off steam and enjoying each other. Bedrooms were more serious places.

Or did the shimmer of nerves come from the change in him? His grip had gone firm and commanding, his voice no-nonsense, and he was suddenly doing rather than checking first. He was the über-cop, the super-ranger, the guy who, when he had burned out on saving one chunk of the world had retreated to protect another.

She was a liberated female, a warrior, the best she could be. And as he carried her into a simply furnished bedroom lit by a dimmer light turned low, tossed her on the bed and followed her down to cover her moisture-slicked body with his own, she was hotter for him than she had ever been for any other man, under any other situation.

His muscular bulk made her feel small and delicate, and when he levered himself up on one elbow to look down at her with fierce heat in his eyes, her blood leaped right back to boiling, though they had had each other only minutes earlier. His look was a challenge, a dare, and it had her reaching for him.

He caught her wrists and guided her hands to the spindles of the headboard. "Not this time."

She would have argued, but he kissed the words away, traced a finger down the center of her body and made her arch into him, helpless beneath the sudden heat, the maelstrom of sensation brought by his tongue and his touch, and the leashed strength she sensed him containing as his legs twined with hers.

Her better sense told her to let go of the spindles and give as good as she got, keeping them on the same level with each other. But the inciting stroke of his fingertips teased her senses and the promise that lit his eyes when he broke the kiss and moved down her body held her in place.

He cupped one breast and had her arching against him, then took her nipple into his mouth, wringing a moan from deep in her throat. Her body heated and throbbed. Pleasure coiled inside her as she tightened her fingers around the headboard spindles and hung on for the ride.

The soft bedspread had bunched up beneath them; he pulled it free and stroked her with it, blotting her face and pushing back her wet hair, then moving down her body, alternately drying and kissing her. All the while, he whispered hot praise and dark suggestions that stirred her to the point of madness.

The sun had set, turning the world dark and making it feel as if they were the only two people on Earth. Danger still lurked outside, but the need for him—and the temptation to let him take charge—was far more immediate. He reared over her, settling back on his haunches to scrub a corner of the bedspread through his thick, dark hair, down across his shoulders and broad chest, and down farther, to where his shaft emerged from its nest of dark curls, ruddy and engorged.

She feasted on the sight of him, shifting almost without volition to rub her thighs together as he tossed the bedspread aside and bent over her.

Her senses spun and her insides clenched when he kissed her stomach, her navel, the point of her hip. Someone moaned—she thought it might have been her, but couldn't be sure. She wasn't sure of anything anymore; her whole world hinged on the touch of his lips and tongue as he moved down and settled himself between her legs.

The sight of his dark head down there made her breath go thin and the contrast of his skin against hers shot flames searing through her. Then he slicked his tongue through her folds, and every part of her clenched in a sudden surge of pleasure that had her bowing back on the mattress with an inarticulate cry.

He rasped something low in his throat—a curse, maybe, or a plea—and did it again. And again. When she strained against him, trying to move, to speed things up, he held her in place with his weight and strength, and kept going—licking, lapping, nuzzling, *taking.*

The breath backed up in her throat as he stripped her defenses and broke through to a place of pure sensation. She responded to him without inhibition or boundaries, no thought of yesterday or tomorrow. He brought her to the edge of release again and again with his mouth and hands, until the pleasure burned her, consumed her, knotted her body tight and left her sobbing with pleasure.

Her hands cramped on the spindles; her body burned for his. She was gasping, babbling pleas and demands that went unheeded until, finally, he looked up at her, his eyes sharp, bright and a little wild. Voice rattling in his chest, he grated, "Now."

"God, yes, now."

He moved up her body. His skin was hot on hers; his scent had become theirs, and was laced with sex.

She was tight all over, needy and greedy. And when he came down atop her, pressing her into the mattress with his hard, solid weight, she couldn't take it anymore. She tore her hands from the headboard and dug her fingers into his hips as he positioned himself at her center, the thick head of his erection just nudging her opening, which was slick and wet, and pulsed for him.

He kissed her long and deep, then broke the kiss, pressed his furnace-hot cheek to hers, and whispered her name as he thrust home, filling her in a single strong, possessive surge.

In an instant, his hard flesh was seated far more deeply, more intimately than before. He surrounded her inside and out, pinned her, possessed her.

Then he fixed his eyes on her and she found herself trapped in their green depths, laid bare by their intensity as he withdrew slowly, then thrust home. The first plunge wrung a gasp from her, the second had a groan rattling deep in his chest. He dropped his head, pressed his cheek to hers, slid into her with delicious friction.

She was laid flat and open beneath him, but moved when and where she could, digging in and meeting his thrusts. His breath was a roar, hers a sob. If she had been on the edge of an orgasm before, now she leaped to a new plateau entirely, one that was huge, breathtaking and scary. Nothing existed except the two of them and a bed behind bulletproof glass as he drove her up toward an impossible pinnacle, one she had never before glimpsed.

She clung to him, anchoring herself to his shoulders, pressing her lips to the scarred indentation where the bullet had gone in. Misplaced terror flashed at the thought that he could have died, that she wouldn't ever have known this, known him. That brought a warning buzz, quickly lost beneath the enormity of the breathless pause that presaged orgasm.

Her body tightened, sensation rushing inward to gather at the place where he stroked her inside and out. He touched all the right spots at once, their joined flesh slick with excitement, and…and…

The world paused. Held its breath.

And she went over the edge.

A shuddering cry escaped from her, mirroring the all-consuming, wrenching fist of her orgasm. It defied logic and boundaries. She bowed into him, gasped against his sweat-slicked flesh as the radiating throbs of pleasure went on and on, sent higher by his harsh groan and three quick thrusts, then higher still when he stiffened against her and came whispering her name in a voice that was filled with awe, approval and satisfaction.

He shuddered, and bucked as her flesh milked him, the echoes of her pleasure prolonging his.

Then, even after things leveled off and their bodies began to cool, they stayed wrapped together, her arms around his shoulders, her ankles locked behind him, their faces pressed together.

Then he backed off and looked down at her, and where before there had been a challenge in his eyes, now there was only a profound tenderness that shifted something inside her.

He opened his mouth to speak, but then just stopped and shook his head. "Later," he whispered, and dropped a kiss to her brow. He rearranged them, nudging her onto her side and fitting her into the curve of his body, then pulling the bedclothes up and over them.

She let him fuss, ignoring the nerves that churned over how far she had let him in, how much she had let go. Instead, she told herself to enjoy the moment, and the man. She would deal with the rest of it later. Tonight was tonight...and for tonight, she wanted to belong entirely to him.

THE NEXT MORNING, GIGI awoke from a fractured jumble of dreams and plunged directly into sensations that were entirely different yet equally terrifying: body heat behind her, an arm across her waist, the pleasurable ache that came from a sex-filled night, her feet pressing atop those of her lover...

Her lover. Matthew H. Blackthorn. Oh, God.

The dreams—an amalgam of the crashed Jeep, the fleeing truck and the imagined scene of a furniture truck slamming into his mother's minivan—cluttered her mind as she rolled to face him.

He woke when she moved, going tense and alert for

a second and then easing, cracking one green eye with an expression that said, *Ah, it's you. No threat.*

But although she might not be on his threat radar, she couldn't say the reverse. Because as she lay there with her head pillowed on his arm and her feet still pressed atop his, she badly wanted to snuggle into him, tuck her head beneath his chin and pretend the world outside didn't exist. More, she could already feel herself storing away the small moments, the details that didn't matter when the sex was just for fun.

She knew how his eyes went dark when he was aroused, how his voice rasped on her name when he climaxed. She knew how he smelled and tasted; how he moved with animal grace one moment and a cop's blunt get-it-done attitude in the next; how he drove like a maniac but would always keep his passenger safe, or die trying.

"No regrets," he said quietly, his eyes steady on hers. It wasn't a question; it was an order. And part of her wanted to go along with him. Because if she could convince herself there was nothing to regret, that she hadn't truly given herself over to him last night, then everything would be okay.

She closed her eyes and whispered inwardly: *You're fine. You're whole. You can handle this.* But instead of confidence came the images of the Jeep, the truck speeding away, brake lights flashing.

It repeated in slow motion: the…truck…speeding… away.

Shock seared through her as she realized what she had seen, what her brain was trying to tell her. Her eyes flew open. "Holy crap. I didn't see it before, but now that I'm more relaxed," she rushed on, not waiting to look hard at the source of that relaxation, "I'm seeing the truck driving away… And I caught a partial plate number."

He stared at her for a three-count, expression unreadable. Then he nodded. "Call it in and let's get moving."

And just like that, their night was over. It was tomorrow, and they had a case to solve.

Chapter Thirteen

Matt drained the hot tub, stuck his clothes in the dryer and generally pulled the place back together while Alyssa ran the plates.

Any thoughts he might've had of a breakfast of eggs and toast with a side of "hey, that got pretty intense last night" had been shot to hell by the break in the case, but maybe that was for the best.

In the clearer-headed light of day, the mind-blowing sex they'd shared didn't change the fact that she had her sights set elsewhere and he didn't have his set on much of anything. In fact, he flat-out hated the idea of her joining a hazardous response team.

Not because she wouldn't be good at it, but because she would be great at it, and there was no way in hell he could wave her off to work and then wonder if she was coming back. The fact that he could picture himself doing just that—and imagine it driving him nuts—just proved he had gotten himself in way too deep last night and needed to back off, fast.

Meanwhile, Gigi was acting as if it was no big deal. He might have been annoyed if he hadn't seen the hint of a plea at the back of her eyes, the well-hidden desperation that said she wasn't any more comfortable with how things had gone than he was, and they should just leave it alone.

Her phone rang in the bedroom, where she was getting dressed in Chelsea's spare clothes.

"It's Alyssa," she called. "I'm putting her on speaker."

"Thanks." He moved into the bedroom doorway and leaned in, looking at the phone rather than Gigi, yet very aware of the sidelong look she shot him.

After the hellos were out of the way, Alyssa said, "Assuming these guys were dumb enough—or ballsy enough—not to switch out the plates, there's only one truck that matches the description and your partial."

"The guys in the truck were amateurs," Matt said with total certainty. "I'm not sure if they're the same ones who went after Tanya or torched the station, but these guys didn't shoot or drive like pros."

"Who's the registered owner of the truck?" Gigi asked. She had one hip propped on the edge of the mattress, as if trying to prove to herself that it was no biggie that they had shared the bed.

"Alex MacDonald. He's a sometimes handyman, always troublemaker who lives near the arena and has a fondness for off-track betting and the occasional hunting trip."

Gigi glanced at him. "Did he come through Station Fourteen?"

"If he did, he didn't make enough of a fuss for me to remember his name. I'd check the records, but…"

"They're torched."

"Right." Even with the fire threat, there hadn't seemed

to be any reason to store copies of the hiking permits online. Most of the people who came through Station Fourteen only lasted a few days, a couple of weeks at the outside.

"I'll send you a picture," Alyssa said.

"Do you have him in custody?"

"Jack is on his way over to his place right now. I—hang on. Tucker's calling in on the other line. I'm going to put you on hold. Be right back." Alyssa clicked off.

That left Matt in the bedroom doorway, Gigi on the bed and a huge elephant in the room, sitting between them.

He told himself to leave it alone, then surprised the hell out of himself by saying, "If I asked you out to dinner once this was over, what would you say?"

From the look on her face, he had surprised the hell out of her, too. Her eyes widened and new color touched her cheeks, but he wasn't sure if that was from pleasure or something else. Then her lips curved, though the expression didn't quite reach her eyes. "When this is over, why don't you ask me and we'll find out?"

With timing so perfect he suspected she had been listening in, Alyssa said, "I'm back. Jack says Alex MacDonald is in the wind, his apartment pretty close to stripped. Cassie is off on a call, so Tucker is going to pick me up and run me over to the apartment to process what's left."

"Are you sure—" Gigi began.

"I'm sure I'm going to lose it if I don't do *something* other than sit on my rapidly spreading butt and coordinate calls and manpower," Alyssa snapped. Then, a little calmer, she said, "The apartment is locked down and there's no off-road bouncing around involved in getting there. You'd need some serious firepower to keep me away, because I hate that these bastards came after you two, and it scares me to think they might try again."

"How about Gigi and I meet you there?" Matt asked. "I can discuss a few things with Tucker while you two work the scene." And it would double up on the firepower if it turned out that the apartment was a trap.

"He said you would say that. I'll send you the address. See you when you get here." The line went dead as she clicked off.

Gigi stood and pocketed the phone, then smoothed her palms down the borrowed pants, which were a little too big. "I'm ready to leave when you are."

"One minute." Going on instinct, making the sort of split-second decision that used to be second nature, he crossed to her, cupped a hand around the back of her neck and laid his lips on hers.

She stiffened and brought her hands up, he thought to push him away. But instead she curled her fingers into his T-shirt and pulled him closer, opening her mouth beneath his.

Heat seared straight through his gut at the touch of her tongue and the taste of her, which was instantly familiar yet still stunningly new. He crowded closer, so their bodies aligned, and his flesh hardened in moments, though he should have been sated.

He couldn't get enough of her. He buried his hands in her hair, ran his tongue along the rim of her ear, tugged at the studs with his teeth and made her moan. Then he eased away, brushing her hair behind her ears and watching how the shorter half of it fell forward once more. "Okay. Now I'm ready to go."

No regrets.

As GIGI FOLLOWED ALYSSA into MacDonald's apartment, which was a small second floor one-bedroom in a dingy three-floor apartment building in a not very nice section of town, she was still debating how much—if anything—to tell her friend about what had happened with Matt.

But the moment the door closed behind them, shutting out the two uniforms stationed in the hallway, Alyssa faced her, crossed her arms atop Baby McDermott and said implacably, "Okay, sister. Spill it."

"I… Darn it, you were listening in on the phone the whole time."

"I caught the end of it, anyway. Sue me." Her eyes gleamed. "What happened with you two last night?"

"Aren't we supposed to be processing a scene?" Gigi took a pointed look around, though admittedly there didn't seem to be much of a scene to process. The apartment had been stripped back to bare walls and plain furniture, with nothing personal that she could see.

"Yep. And it'll go much faster if you confess, so we can get started." Alyssa paused. "Or you can tell me to mind my own business."

Gigi winced. "Ouch. Low blow."

"I'll start. You slept together. That's obvious, given the way he was looking at you just now."

"I…" To Gigi's horror, her eyes filled with tears. "Oh, crap." She spun away, mortified, feeling her control start to slip. Aware that Alyssa was coming over, knowing that a kind word might break her, she held up a hand. "Don't. Please."

"Sorry. I'm pregnant, which means I can do pretty much what I want and I'll be forgiven." The blonde wrapped her arms around Gigi, sandwiching Baby Mc-Dermott between them, and said, "You don't have to be a hero with me. Not ever."

A big sob welled up, jamming Gigi's throat. She held on for another few seconds, then let go, sagging against Alyssa and giving herself permission to lose it and give in to the shakes that had eluded her the night before.

Her friend hung on. "It's okay, kiddo. Whatever's going on, it's going to be okay."

She sucked in a shuddering breath as tears scalded her eyes, but to her surprise, that was all that happened. After a moment, she lost the overwhelming urge to wail, and the tightness in her throat eased. A minute after that, she could breathe again.

Letting out a shaky laugh, she straightened away from Alyssa. "Well. That was anticlimactic. I guess…I think… Wow. It's been a pretty intense few days."

Alyssa pressed her hands into her lower back and leaned against a corner of a ratty couch that looked like a few more fibers wouldn't make any difference one way or the other. "Would that be the part where you dove back into a burning building, made it through a car chase or spent the night with Matt in the 'safe' house?" The finger quotes said she knew exactly what kind of a house it was.

"All of it." Gigi's cheeks heated. "And you could've warned me about the cabin."

"Would it have changed anything?"

"Maybe." But honesty compelled her to admit, "Probably not." She and Matt had been on a collision course. It would've happened with or without the ambience.

"So. You going to give a pregnant lady some details?"

"Only if said pregnant lady is working while we talk." Given that MacDonald had taken the time to strip the place bare, logic said that it probably wouldn't yield anything useful. But instinct itched along her spine, telling her that there was something…

Or maybe not. Maybe her emotions had screwed with her instincts. Wasn't that what Matt had been implying when he mentioned the two guys on his team who'd had things on their mind the day of the bank robbery?

It didn't escape her that his point jibed with the Lynd protocol: one thing at a time. Work, then family. Mixing the two was risky, especially if you wanted to be the best at both.

Alyssa nodded. "How about you get started and I'll catch up. Better yet, I'll observe your highly trained technique."

"Wow. You're really working it, aren't you?" Gigi sent her a look. "Or are you feeling crappy again?"

"Little bit of both." She nudged her field kit with a toe. "I'm waiting."

Gigi put on her protective gear and got to work, first taking a tour of the apartment, looking for obvious stuff and snapping some overview photos, and then coming back to the main room.

Alyssa sent her a look, then pointedly drummed her fingers atop Baby McDermott. "Still waiting."

Starting with a banged up wooden desk that had a

layer of dust on it with a laptop-shaped void off to one side, Gigi took more pictures with a ruler for scale, and then used a shoeprint-size piece of transfer paper to take a print of the laptop. She wasn't hopeful that it would lead to anything, though. Thanks to the TV shows, the bad guys had gotten way better at cleaning up after themselves. *Hello, CSI effect.*

Finally, she said, "I called my mom last night to tell her what was going on."

Alyssa raised an eyebrow. "And?"

"I couldn't tell her about it. Any of it." Gigi went through the drawers, which held nothing but lint and crumbs. "She just finally started getting behind the idea of me trying to get into the accelerated training program. Mostly because it's a tangible goal that involves testing and competition, which she gets, even if she doesn't understand why this is what I want to do."

"Dangerous professions can be harder on the family than the individual. The individual chooses the job, chooses the risk. The family members don't always get a vote."

Hearing a tone, Gigi glanced over. "You and Tucker make it work, and so do Cassie and Seth."

"Three of the four of us are analysts. And while we see more action than the norm, being in Bear Claw—or in Seth's case, a field office—the action is still the exception. As for Fax and Chelsea…well, they're different. He sponsored her into the agency, made her his partner. But…" She shook her head. "He worked under a female superior for a long time, which I think makes him more ready to accept Chelsea being in the field with him."

Gigi let out a soft sigh. "Whereas Matt has spent most of his life trying to protect the world from itself."

"He could change."

Now it was Gigi's turn to raise an eyebrow.

"Okay, maybe not." Alyssa paused. "Where did you guys leave things?"

With a kiss that had shot right to the top of her top ten, one that had made her feel strong yet feminine, like she was the supercop's girl, the center of his world. "With a 'maybe' on going out to dinner after this case is wrapped up and things go back to normal."

Alyssa made a face. "Which one of you was doing the most backpedaling?"

"I'd say we were about even." Gigi abandoned the desk and moved to the couch, which was the only other large piece of furniture in the cramped sitting area.

Alyssa shifted over to lean on the desk, moving slowly, while Gigi gave the carpet a quick scan—wincing at the profusion of fibers, most if not all of which would be totally useless.

Part of an analyst's job was making judgment calls about what to collect and what to leave behind. Each piece of evidence she selected represented dollars, man hours, storage space and analytics.

One of the things that made her very good at what she did was her instincts. Normally, she could look at a scene and know, at a gut-check level, what to take. Now, though, her instincts were humming, but they weren't telling her anything. It wasn't just Alyssa being there, either. Her head wasn't in the game.

She used a small flashlight to look under the couch, trying to make out anything useful amid the dust rats.

"When I woke up this morning, I thought to myself that if he asked me to turn down the academy and stay here with him, I would seriously consider it." She was ashamed even saying it aloud. "I've known the guy—really known him, I mean, not just to the point of avoiding each other in the hallway—for what, seventy-two hours? And we've been in each other's faces—and not in the good way—for more than half that time. So it's ridiculous for me to even think…" She shook her head. "It's ridiculous."

"Maybe, but there's such a thing as love at first sight."

Gigi snorted. "Lust at first sight, maybe, but not love. We're not… It's not like that." But she glanced over. "Was it that way for you and Tucker?"

"No way. We met. We danced. We hooked up. We realized, belatedly, that we were going to be working together. And big, bad Tucker McDermott, the original 'I'm a rolling stone, just passing through' didn't want anything to do with a girl who wanted to put down roots, so we spent the next few months snarling at each other." She shook her head. "No, I'm thinking of Fax and Chelsea, actually. When she met him, he was posing as a convict and had just helped al-Jihad himself break out of the ARX prison. He was on the job, deep undercover…and they got one good look at each other, and fell hard."

"Oh." Gigi had to swallow past the wistful lump in her throat. "Well. We already know Fax is a special case. And I'm the 'doesn't want to put down roots' factor in this equation. I still have things I want to do before I settle down."

"Why does it have to be settling? Why can't it be making a choice of one thing you want over something else you want? Or, better yet, finding a way to have them both."

Pulling the cushions off the sofa with more force than was probably necessary, Gigi probed the cracks and found the usual gnarly assortment of crumbs, old food, wrappers, coins and other garbage. "That's not the way it works in my family."

"So be the black sheep and do your own thing."

"Been there, done that." Gigi flicked at her earrings and hair.

"Those are little things."

"The job isn't."

"Maybe, but you're still doing the 'got to be the best' thing they're so into." Alyssa shifted, wincing.

Gigi's instincts flared. "You're not in labor, are you?"

"God, no. I'd be screaming my head off. And don't change the subject."

"Do you swear you're not in labor?"

"I swear. Seriously. Now let's move on."

Gigi felt her way along the back of the sofa, where things sometimes got wedged and forgotten. "Look, I know my family is whacked-out, okay? In a good way, maybe, but whacked-out nonetheless. I know there's no law that says I have to be in the top whatever percentile of the universe…but what if I want to be? My parents gave me all these great opportunities, so why not use them to shoot for the moon? I want to be on a hazardous response team. I want the adrenaline rush. I want to save lives and be an über-cop, not just date one." Love one.

Marry one and spend the rest of her life waking up as she had that morning, wrapped up in him and pleasantly satiated from their lovemaking. Maybe even riding herd on a couple of green-eyed—

Whoa, back up. Getting in way too deep there. She could feel the urgency building, the need to see him again, even though he and Tucker were just outside.

"An über-cop?" Alyssa's voice was amused.

"Oh, shut up. You know what I mean. I've got goals that are mine, not my family's, and I don't want to give them up."

"Has he asked you to?"

"Not yet." But he would. If things went any further between them, she would eventually have to decide between him and the job. She knew that deep down in her soul. "Right now, *I'm* more the problem than he is. I've got this thing going on inside me that I don't like. At all. When I'm not with him, I'm thinking about him, obsessing over him, both the good stuff and the bad." Even saying it aloud made her feel shaky and weak. "Then when I *am* with him, I go back and forth between wanting to tear his clothes off with my teeth, and wanting to slap at him because I hate feeling this way and it's his fault. Only it isn't. It's *mine*."

"Oh, Gigi. Honey."

She wound down, breathing hard, and realized she was crouched over the sofa, glaring into its sprung interior like a madwoman. Looking up, she found Alyssa watching her, wide-eyed. "See? He's making me crazy. Strike that. I'm making myself crazy over him." She pushed to her feet, wanting to pace, but not letting herself because she had a *job* to do, damn it.

"Gigi—"

"I hate this. I must look completely—" *Insane,* she started to say, but then broke off as she flashed on the prior morning, when Matt had yelled at Ian over the mayor's shenanigans…and looked completely insane doing it. "Oh, for crap's sake." She started laughing helplessly, almost hysterically as she realized she was doing the same damn thing—yelling at a friend because she couldn't deal with the amount of emotion he could pull from her. "You've got to be kidding me. We're like fertilizer and fuel, functional on our own, but put us together and *pow,* stuff gets blown up."

"I have no idea what you're talking about."

"I know. It's okay, really. I'm not losing it." She took a deep breath. "I'm just figuring a few things out." She put the sofa cushions back, then stood in the center of the room and did a careful three-sixty turn, looking for anything else that pinged on her radar screen, even if this particular scene might just be about going through the motions.

"A few things," Alyssa repeated. "Like the fact that you two are good for each other."

"Ha-ha. Try that one again. More like we set each other off, and… Well, what have we got here?" Her instincts suddenly kicked hard and she went on point. "Does that look like blood to you over there on the doorframe? Looks like blood to me."

The rusty smear hadn't been immediately obvious because the rest of the place was pretty filthy, but when she looked at it from exactly the right angle, there was a handprint pattern to the grime on the doorframe leading to the bathroom.

Senses humming, she approached the spot, ignoring the funky smell coming from the room beyond.

Alyssa came up behind her. "Looks pretty new."

The blood was dry and rusty, but the imprint was crisp, unsmudged by later traffic.

"Could've been from yesterday," Gigi agreed. "Maybe from the guy Matt shot, or someone who tried to stop the bleeding." Which not only suggested the men had been in the apartment very recently, it made the bathroom the next obvious place to search.

She took pictures of the handprint and then lifted it and took a couple of DNA swabs. She handed off the evidence for Alyssa to bag and tag while she kept going, her pulse drumming a little with the high that came from being on the verge of finding a piece to add to the puzzle.

The bathroom itself was small and scuzzy, an abstract study in cracked porcelain and rodent droppings. It, too, had been stripped of its personal items, but the trash basket held a few scraps of wax-coated paper at the bottom. "Looks like someone did some first aid in here."

"More blood?"

"Pieces of bandage wrappers. There's no obvious blood—given how good they were about picking up after themselves elsewhere, they probably bleached it to nuke the DNA." But that was okay, she had the handprint. She should be able to lift enough DNA from it to give Cassie something to work with.

After taking more photos, she picked up the trash basket and shook it to move the bandage wrappers around and see if there was anything more interesting beneath.

A piece of paper unstuck itself from the bottom of the can and fluttered to the floor.

"Hello." There went her instincts again.

Alyssa poked her head in. "Got something?"

"Maybe." Gigi took some photos and made a couple of notes, tightening up her chain of evidence in case the scrap of paper turned out to be something useful. Then she reached down and picked it up, handling it as carefully as she could.

For a second, disappointment threatened when she saw that it was just another bandage wrapper, this one mostly intact. But then she saw the bloody thumbprint on one edge and writing on the other side, and adrenaline sizzled through her. "It's a note. Numbers. Letters. And a date and time." She looked up, blood draining from her face. "Whatever it is, it's happening in less than two hours."

Chapter Fourteen

Matt took one look at the note Gigi had spread out on a rickety desk and said, "The middle numbers are GPS coordinates." At Gigi's frown, he added, "It's a military notation scheme, not civilian."

"Alex MacDonald was in the National Guard," Alyssa put in.

He caught Gigi's quick glance, but got busy pulling out his phone and keying the sequence into the GPS feature. "Who do you have that's good at codes?" The number-letter sequences almost made sense, but not really.

She photographed the scrap of paper. "I'll send it to a friend, see if she has any suggestions."

"If you're cool with it, you could hit up Ian, too. He's good at puzzles." At her nod, he rattled off the number. His GPS was taking forever. "Come on, you bugger. Load already."

"Yeah," Tucker put in drily, "Talking to it always helps." He stood a few paces away with Alyssa, who was propped up against the sofa and looked more than a little pasty. Tucker, too, was pretty drawn all of a sudden.

"Everything okay?"

"I'd be lots better if people stopped asking me if I'm okay," Alyssa snapped, then closed her eyes and shook her head. "Sorry. Crabby."

"You've earned it, I'd say." But he caught Gigi's worried look, and his gut churned slowly at the realization that as a team, they were batting a thousand on the distraction factors. "Look, if you two want to head out—" His phone rang, interrupting. He glared at the stalled GPS transfer and stabbed the button to answer. "Blackthorn here."

"We got MacDonald," Jack said, satisfaction plain in his voice. "Idiot ran his truck off the road heading up into the backcountry."

"Hang on," Matt said. "I'm putting you on speaker. Go ahead."

"One of the search parties found him and sat on him until I got here. He's light-headed from blood loss and a fever, and he's singing like a freaking canary. That's the good news. The bad news is what he's telling us: apparently he and a half dozen other local thugs, along with some out-of-town muscle, have been keeping those fires down at Sectors Five and Six going in order to tie up air support and keep the rangers focused downhill. The break-ins were theirs, too—partly for entertainment and profit, partly to mix things up and, again, to keep attention off other parts of the park."

Matt's blood iced with fury at MacDonald and the others—and whoever was controlling them. They'd destroyed thousands of acres and caused numerous casualties for nothing more than distraction.

But part of his fury was self-directed. He hadn't

caught on. The bastards had torched his station, yet he hadn't made the leap to the wildfires.

A hand touched his, making him aware that he had grabbed onto a nearby doorframe, was clutching it so tightly his knuckles were white, his fingers cramping. Gigi. He knew it was her without looking, felt the sizzle in her touch, the compassion.

But when he looked down into her eyes, he only saw annoyance.

"You don't have a crystal ball, remember?" She tapped his bloodless knuckles. "I don't care how good your hindsight is, you couldn't have seen this one coming. So just take a breath, cut yourself some slack, and focus on what we can do something about, which is what's happening right now, and what we can plan in the next couple of hours."

And the damn thing was, she was right. In three days, she had gotten to know him better than…hell, anyone in his life except, perhaps, for Ian.

He took a deep breath and nodded. "Thanks," he said quietly, privately. Then, raising his voice, he said, "Sorry, Jack. You were saying?"

"Here's the thing. MacDonald doesn't know who he's working for or why this guy—it's a guy's voice on the phone, that's all I'm getting—wants our attention on the foothills. Or if he does know, he's not saying." He paused. "Apparently Tanya saw and took something she shouldn't have, and the voice on the phone told Mac-Donald and a couple of his buddies to shut her up and destroy the evidence. The next thing they know, Matt and Gigi are on the list, too, because they're getting too close. And then…wait, hang on."

Voices murmured in the background, and then Jack cursed viciously.

Returning to the call, he said, "Okay, forget that stuff. You guys need to get on this, *fast*. Apparently MacDonald was headed up to meet up with the others and get new marching orders. They're going to hit Sector Nine this afternoon."

Matt's blood went from ice to a vicious boil. "Sons. Of. Bitches. If Nine goes, the whole damn park goes." Then it wouldn't matter what Proudfoot sold or didn't sell—it would all be worthless char.

"The meeting," Gigi said urgently. She tapped the note. "That's got to be it."

A ping sounded from his phone, indicating that the download had been completed. "About freaking time." He grabbed the phone and said to Jack, "Call us if you get anything more out of MacDonald." Toggling over to the other screen, he took a look at the map the GPS coordinates had pulled up, and nearly groaned. "Perfect. That's just freaking perfect."

"Where are they meeting?" Tucker asked.

"The Forgotten." Matt looked around the room, trying to stow his emotions and deal with the problem right in front of him, namely how they could get out there in time. "We need a damn chopper." But the functional birds were all out at Sectors Five and Six, and most of them were limping—there wasn't enough time to get one out to the Forgotten.

"What about Fax's helicopter?" Gigi said. "The one with all the bells and whistles?"

"That might actually work," Tucker said, surprised.

"Last I checked, it was at the old airfield near Station Eight, on the west side."

Alyssa was already on her phone. "Chelsea? We need your help. Well, actually, we need your chopper and your pilot."

"Come on." Matt said, heading for the door. "We'll meet them there." Entering a sort of highly functional haze that wasn't quite his old crisis response mode, he hit redial, and when Williams answered, said, "If you can pawn off MacDonald, meet us at the old airstrip just past Ranger Station Eight. Wait. What's your closest station right now?"

"Um. Ten, I think. I'm pretty far up."

"Good. Go there first. Someone will meet you with guns. Grab them and meet me at the airstrip."

He powered past the uniforms and hit the street, then turned back to Tucker. "We'll see you there?" He was asking about more than just a rendezvous.

"Absolutely," Alyssa said. When Tucker turned on her, she glared right back. "I'm. Fine."

Leaving them to their fight, he ducked into the rental as Gigi launched herself into the other side and went for her seat belt. Her eyes gleamed. "Finally, a big foam finger."

She terrified him.

Tabling that for the moment, he put in a call to his quarters, hoping someone was there. Bert answered, "Station Fourteen."

For a second Matt couldn't say anything, as the sound of the older ranger's familiar voice slammed home how far he was from the man he'd been just a few days ago. He didn't wish himself back up there, wasn't pining for his solitude. He wanted to get to the airstrip and be right in the thick of things.

He glanced at Gigi, who was on her phone, trying to get some birds diverted to fly over Sector Nine. From the looks of it, she wasn't having much luck.

"Boss? That you?"

"Yeah. Sorry, Bert. Look, I'll catch you up later. Right now, I need you to patch me through to Ten, ASAP. Get me Harvey if he's there. Once you've done that, get all of your volunteers headed for Sector Nine. There's a chance someone's going to try to torch it."

"They do that, and the whole place is toast."

"Which is why we need to make sure it doesn't happen. So get me Harvey, and get the others moving."

"On it."

As Matt steered the rental onto the highway leading out to the city and passed a big sign for the state park, the head of Station Ten came on the line. "Blackthorn? Harvey here."

"There's a cop headed your way, name is Williams. He needs whatever serious firepower you've got, with full ammo. Hook him up and then spread the word that you may have firebugs incoming to Sector Nine within the next few hours. I'll get you descriptions and more details when I can, but until then, do your best. Watch the roads, the skies, whatever it takes."

"Blackthorn, what the devil is going on?"

"Someone is trying to keep our attention off the Forgotten. That's all I know." How the mayor—or his buyer—figured into it was something they would need to look long and hard at. Later.

Harvey cursed and cut the connection. But he was a good man, a good ranger; he would get the job done.

Gigi ended her call, shaking her head. "Maybe. That's all I could get out of them. A maybe. They didn't seem to want to hear that if Sector Nine goes, it won't matter that Five and Six are burning—the whole damn place is going to go up." She was tight-lipped and grim, but her anger shifted to something more personal as she looked at him. "It's not a very big helicopter."

He nodded. "Pilot plus three if you skip the copilot. Maybe one more if you get real friendly. She's built for speed and fuel efficiency, but the trade-off is a low payload, and not much space."

Her brows drew together. "You'd better not be thinking about leaving me behind. This is my case and I'm your partner. *Right?*"

He hesitated. "Tucker's got the final say. He's got the rank, not me."

But Matt was going to do his damnedest to make sure that she didn't get anywhere near the Forgotten.

Chapter Fifteen

Gigi fumed in silence for the rest of the drive. But when they pulled onto the deserted airstrip and came into view of the sleek black agency chopper, she said quietly, "I've earned this one and you know it."

Matt cut a hard-eyed look at her. "Life isn't fair."

"You said the pilot plus four. That's you, Jack, Fax and me." When he glared, she just lifted her chin. "I'm a better shot than Jack."

"Not by much. And you forgot Tucker."

"No, I didn't." They both knew he wasn't getting on that helicopter. Even if the detective was willing to leave Alyssa, he was too far off his game thinking about the baby to be any good to anyone right now.

Matt parked out of range of the rotor sweep and they got out of the rental just as Tucker's SUV rolled into view.

Gigi came around the hood of the car and squared off opposite Matt. Her blood was running high with righteous indignation, but that didn't stop her from feeling the inevitable skitter of heat that hit her whenever she looked at him. It was stronger than ever now, and she was still storing up those damn details: she was conscious of the tight worry in his expression, the stark determination that wasn't the cop or the ranger, it was, quite simply, *him*.

"Gigi, please don't do this," he said quietly. "Not now. Later, after you're all the way trained, I'll…" He trailed off with a small shake of his head.

"You can't even say it, can you?" Her heart sank. She had known that it would probably come down to this between them. She just hadn't expected it to be so soon. She wasn't ready for the flameout yet.

Tucker parked nearby and climbed out of the SUV. Alyssa's door opened, but it was a moment before her feet appeared. Gigi was deeply worried for her friend, but she couldn't afford to let Matt win on this one. Not if she intended to hold her own in whatever happened between them next.

"This isn't about us," Matt said urgently. His eyes were stark. "It's a tactical decision. Yes, you're a sharp-shooter, but you don't have any actual live firefighting experience, and we're not going to be dealing with just MacDonald this time. We don't have any intel, and there's no way to get a satellite feed in time. We're going in blind, with no clue what we're going to find when we get there. Admit it, that's not the sort of scenario you've trained on."

He was right, of course. Hazardous response, especially in the city, was all about collecting information before and during the op, and using it to make the best plans and decisions. This, on the other hand, was going to be a "hit the ground and go" scenario, with the added risks that brought.

She took a step toward him, until they were close

enough to touch each other, close enough to kiss. "Nobody is going to watch your back the way I will," she said with quiet determination. "If the roles were reversed, and I was the one who had to go because it was my territory, you'd be fighting for a spot on that chopper."

"I would kill for it," he said simply.

His stark words and the punch of emotion in his voice put a lump in her throat. "Then you know how I feel."

"Fine. Great. How about picturing this: we're on the ground, there are men shooting at us—real, live men, not cardboard cutouts—and I'm so damned terrified for you that I'm not watching my own six. Which is fine, because you've got my back. But I'm also not on top of what's going on with the others. We get scattered, pinned down, freaking *gunned* down because I can't think straight while you're out there."

She didn't know how so much aching tenderness could coexist with so much pain. But somehow it did, sliding through her and leaving her bleeding even as she wished she could back down and give him what he wanted.

She couldn't, though. In the end, it turned out she was a Lynd all the way, after all.

Reaching up, she smoothed the neckline of his T-shirt. "This is who I am, Matt. This is what I want. If you can't accept me being out in the field, right now, today, then…" she faltered, but made herself keep going, "then don't bother calling when this is over."

"This isn't about a date," he grated. "There's already way more than that between us, and you damn well know it. Why do we need to do this right now? We can take time to figure this out and find some sort of compromise we can both live with. Preferably *not* in the middle of an op."

His face was stark, his eyes as close to begging as they got. Her heart twisted—she wanted to give in to him so badly, but it was that very urge that had her standing her ground. If she gave in now, she would lose a piece of herself. "We can absolutely discuss this later, after *we* finish this op."

Matt raised his voice. "Tucker, as ranking—"

Alyssa gave a low cry, clutched her stomach, and doubled over. She might have gone down, but Tucker was there to catch her shoulders and prop her back up, his touch incredibly gentle, his face simultaneously tender and frustrated beyond words as he said, "Seriously. Are you ready to 'fess up yet, or would a nice helicopter ride feel good right about now?"

"Fine," Alyssa said between gritted teeth.

"Fine, what?"

"I'm. In. Labor." She spaced the words, looking furious, but the moment they were out there, her eyes filled with tears. She looked at him with mingled terror and exhilaration and whispered shakily, "Hey, McDermott. We're going to have a baby."

"Yeah. We are." Tucker turned to Matt, jaw set. "I'm putting you in charge, effective immediately."

Gigi's stomach sank.

"Then here are your orders," Matt said. "Take Alyssa and Gigi back to the city, and don't let either of them out of your sight."

"Matt, please." Gigi grabbed his arm, fingers digging into his solid strength as her instincts warned that she needed to go with him, be with him. "I can handle myself. You know I can."

She saw the things he had learned over the past few days battle it out against history and loss. He shook his head. "I can't. I'm sorry, Gigi. I'm…" He stretched out a hand to her, but when she backed away, he let it drop. To Tucker, he said harshly, "Take her. Watch her. I'm counting on you to…I'm just counting on you. Don't let me down."

Face haggard, Tucker nodded. "We need to go now. We can't wait for the others."

Matt nodded. "Go. They'll be here any minute."

"Matt," Gigi whispered. Her throat ached with the tears she would shed later; her chest burned where her heart had broken. "Please. Let me be *me*."

But he turned away and said harshly, "Get her out of here."

Someone grabbed her arm; she jerked back and raised her fists, then froze when she saw Alyssa. She let down her guard. "Sorry. I'm sorry."

"I know. And I am, too, but we really need to go." She pressed her hands to the sides of her belly. "And I mean now."

Gigi looked back at Matt, met his eyes, and felt his pain as well as her own. "Be careful, damn you." Then she headed for the SUV with Tucker and Alyssa, and she didn't let herself look back.

The next few minutes were a whirl: another contraction hit while she and Tucker were getting Alyssa into the car, and then they were in and moving, with Gigi propping up Alyssa in the backseat and Tucker driving like a man possessed.

Gigi waited until they were past the first hangar and out of Matt's line of sight. Then she said, "Forgive me."

Alyssa craned to look at her. "For what?"

"This." Gigi pulled her Beretta, thumbed the safety and pointed it at Tucker's head. "Pull over."

He didn't even flinch. "I can't, Gigi. He's right. Fax, Jack and the pilot all have loads more training than you do."

"Check your text messages. Jack got hung up at Station Ten and Fax and the pilot are still forty minutes out. They're not going to make it in time." She racked the action. "Pull over. I can't let him do it." *And please don't make me make this any worse.* She had the perfect hostage right there in her arms.

"Do what?"

"Go after the bastards on his own, flying solo. Literally."

Tucker hit the brake and brought the SUV to a shuddering, screeching stop. He spun toward her, and for a second she thought he was going to come over the seat at her and fight for the gun. But he snapped, "Put the damn gun away and start talking. How many chopper hours does he have?"

"I don't know. But he knew her specs right off the top of his head, and his father died in a helicopter crash. National Guard. My guess is that he got good enough not to be afraid." It was what she would have done.

"I know for damn sure he hasn't flown since he's been here."

"Then let's hope it's like riding a bicycle." She reached for the door.

Alyssa grabbed her arm, fingers digging in. "This is crazy. You can't go. You don't know for sure that he can even fly the thing. And what are you going to do when you get there? He's right—you don't have a plan, intel, enough manpower. It could be suicide!"

Gigi covered Alyssa's hand with her own and squeezed. "I'm not being stupid this time. I'm doing what I need to do. He needs me." Another, more profound sentiment echoed through her, but she kept it to herself.

Alyssa turned weepy eyes on her husband. "Tell her she can't do this. Make it an order. Do *something*."

For a second, he hesitated. Then he hit the locks and opened her door. "Go. You don't have much time."

"Tucker!" Alyssa flared.

"Enough!" he snapped back. "You think I like this? If you hadn't insisted on coming out with me—"

"Stop it, both of you," Gigi said, sharply enough to have them subsiding. She hugged Alyssa tightly, reached up to grip Tucker's shoulder and slipped out of the SUV, then leaned back in to say, "Go have your baby. Let us worry about the other stuff."

"Be careful," Tucker grated. "That's an order."

"I'll do better than that. I'll be good." To Alyssa, she said, "Ten bucks says I get to the hospital before Baby M puts in an in-person appearance." She shut the door and stepped back as Tucker cranked the transmission and peeled away.

Alyssa pressed her face to the window, spreading a hand in farewell, or maybe to wish her luck.

But as she set off through the echoing hangar, hoping to get around behind the sleek black helicopter and use the code Fax had texted her to sneak in through the rear hatch, she heard the sound of rotors and her heart stopped.

Her luck had already run out. She was too late.

MATT HADN'T FLOWN IN nearly eight years and this baby was way more than he'd ever handled before, but she was fairly idiotproof—to the point that a chopper could be, anyway. Between his having chatted up the pilot the other day, and Fax—another lone ranger type— texting him the codes when it became clear that he and the pilot weren't going to make it in time, Matt maneuvered it off the ground without too much trouble.

The chopper wobbled a little, then leveled off and got underway.

He didn't let himself look at the main road to check on the SUV, didn't let himself think about the broken grief on Gigi's face as Tucker and Alyssa had taken her away to safety. Instead, he sent the chopper hurtling toward the Forgotten and did his best to clear his mind.

Half an hour into the forty-five minute flight, when he dropped low and skimmed the treetops, he admitted it was no damned good. His mind wasn't even close to being clear.

All he could think about was her.

He hated that he'd hurt her, hated that he couldn't get past his own hang-ups when it came to her going into the field as a cop, never mind crisis response. Most of all, he hated the way her eyes had gone dead as Alyssa pulled her away, and how his insides had hollowed out at the realization that she had lost faith in him, in them.

"Damn it," he muttered under his breath, and checked the readouts. He was ten minutes out with twenty-five to spare. And with no scanners online, he was going in blind with the simplest of plans: take out any and all vehicles, identify the boss, and grab him.

It sounded simple, but wouldn't be. And he should be thinking about that, not about the woman he'd left behind.

How had things gone so wrong so fast? How had she become so important to him in so little time? It had been less than seventy-two hours since she skidded her ride into the parking lot at Station Fourteen and promptly made him eat his attitude, but in those three days she had gotten under his skin, into his heart. She had changed him, awakened him, made him *feel*.

He didn't want to lose her. But he didn't know how to keep her without losing part of himself.

"Damn it, Gigi," he said aloud. "Why couldn't you have given me this one?"

"Because it would've been the first of many," she said over the thudding engine noise.

He jolted and whipped around, swearing when he found her standing right behind him. His blood fired at the sight of her, a potent combination of fear, anger, desire, tenderness…and reluctant admiration. Because damned if she hadn't somehow doubled back and stowed away on the chopper.

"How did you—" Remembering the rear hatch—and the fact that Fax played by his own rules—he did the math. "I'm going to kill Tucker."

"Don't blame him—I made him do it. At gunpoint, no less."

Putting his attention back on the controls, he snapped, "Sit down and strap in, we're almost there." But as she came forward and fumbled with the copilot's harness, he had to ask, "Why did you come after me?" He thought she had given up on him back at the airstrip.

"Because there was no way in hell I was going to let you fly solo on this one." She glanced over. "Why did you send me away?"

"Because I'd rather watch you walk out than bleed out."

She blanched, but lifted her chin defiantly. "Those aren't the only two options."

"They are the way I see things."

"Then I feel bad for you." She turned deliberately to the panel in front of her, pulled her phone and checked a saved message.

He nearly groaned. "Fax sent you instructions for the guns, too?"

"Just shut up and fly," she said.

He growled low in his throat and thought about stuffing her in a parachute and throwing her out the door. He didn't have the time or altitude, though, so he was going to have to make sure he kept her in one piece, no matter what.

The responsibility was a heavy weight on his shoulders, the pressure a yoke around his neck. His blood burned with anger, his chest was tight with frustration... and he felt acutely, painfully alive.

He wanted to grab her, shake her, kiss her, make love to her. Watching Tucker and Alyssa drag her away from him had been one of the hardest things he had done; thinking it was over had been one of the lowest points of his life. And now, God, he didn't know what to say, how to tell her that this was it for him, she was it. That somehow they were going to have to find a compromise, because he didn't ever want to watch her walk away again. And he damn sure wasn't going to watch her bleed.

Determination firming, he checked his readouts and turned to her just as the chopper crested a low line of trees. "Gigi, I need to—" A shrill bleat cut him off, coming from the console, where a display blinked a warning.

Blood icing, he whipped back to scan the ground below them. Too late, he saw that the "treeline" was camouflage netting strung over a half-dozen tents and twice as many vehicles, ranging from dirt bikes to a huge box trailer hooked to a heavy duty truck.

"There!" she cried, pointing to the smoky trail of a rocket-propelled grenade. It was headed right for them.

For a second, he froze, paralyzed by the thought that he, too, was going to die in a chopper crash, and that he was going to take Gigi with him. Then a second buzzer went off, snapping him straight into a crisis mode that was more intense than any he'd experienced before.

Shouting, he laid the chopper over onto its side and banked, veering sharply up into the sky. "Can you see it?"

She twisted, trying to get a look behind them. "No, I—" A booming thud reverberated through the tiny cabin and she screamed as more warnings shrilled.

Matt's stomach headed for his toes and he swore as the chopper listed heavily, wallowed for a second and then nosed down. As it did, he caught sight of a forest service Jeep sitting beside a river a few miles away from the camouflaged camp, nearly hidden beneath a stone outcropping.

"Matt!"

"I'm trying!" He aimed for the Jeep, but the tail rotor was toast, his control sluggish to nonexistent, and they were too damn low for chutes to be any use. "Hang on!"

Chapter Sixteen

The helicopter crashed into the dry riverbed with a terrible, rending roar of tortured metal, the scream of an overloading engine, and the *whip-whip-whip* of the main rotor blades slamming into the ground and coming apart.

Gigi cried out as the cockpit took a huge, spinning bounce and she was shaken like a ragdoll. Her harness cut into her hips and shoulders, and her stomach couldn't catch up, but all she could do was hang on and pray. As the windshield cracked and the rear door tore free, churning dust and rocks poured in, adding to the chaos.

Then the bulk of the cockpit thudded into something and jolted to a wrenching, shuddering stop. The console surged, spat and died.

"Gigi!" Matt wrenched free of his harness and lurched across to yank at hers.

Her head and stomach were spinning in opposite directions, but she slapped his hands away. "I'm fine."

Then she popped the buckles, pitched into his arms, and let out two wrenching sobs as she clung to him with all her strength. She absolutely, positively was *not* fine.

She was scared and shaken, and her emotions were all over the place. She wanted to push him away, pull him close, scratch at him, shake him, kiss him, hold on to him and never, ever let go.

She was a wreck. And so was their chopper.

He crushed her to him. *"Gigi."* They held each other for a few seconds. Then they pulled apart and he shoved her toward the ripped-open doorway. "Go!"

As if they had practiced it a hundred times, she paused at the opening, crouched and looked low while he went high. She had her Beretta out; he was ready with his Sig Sauer. They shared a look and she went through the doorway, with him right behind her.

Her boots crunched wetly on the riverbed, which had a skim of water running through the rounded stones, a slightly deeper channel in the middle. She stuck to the edge of the narrow canyon, where a slight overhang offered the illusion of safety.

"Head downstream," Matt directed, staying close and keeping his voice low. "We're not that far from the bigger river. Fingers crossed that the Jeep is drivable and the keys are in it."

Miles out of radio range, with the chopper's main systems fried and limited knowledge of its tricks, their best option was going to be to drive to somewhere they could make contact with their team.

Turning downstream and picking up a mile-eating jog, Gigi tossed over her shoulder, "Keys are optional. I can hotwire it if it's still working."

She had the satisfaction of seeing his double take, then a reluctant glint of approval as she turned back and picked up the pace. Holding her gun at the ready as she ran, she scanned their surroundings for two-legged predators as well as others of the clawed or slithering variety. The coast seemed clear, the only sound that of the air moving through the trees.

It wasn't that she'd stopped being scared—the fear was there, and not even buried all that deeply. But at the same time, going fetal wasn't an option, so she was just doing what needed to be done. *Just do it,* she thought, the words taking on the feeling of a Lynd family battle cry.

"Hear that?" he said quietly. "I think we found Tanya's waterfall."

He was right. That wasn't the wind in the trees; they were getting close to the river, and there was a cascade somewhere nearby. Excitement kicked at the sense that the case was finally coming together, though the adrenaline was tempered by the fact that they were cut off from backup.

The rushing roar grew louder, and the canyon took a sharp left, blocking their view. She paused at the turn, waited for Matt to move in close, and then looked low while he went high.

She caught her breath at the sight of a wide, rushing river with elevated banks that suggested it was far from its peak level. Both sides of the river were lined by scrubby trees that looked like an old man's hands— gnarled and bent, with tufts of wiry white fibers growing in strange patches and trailing down. The water churned through a small set of rapids just downstream from them, and maybe five hundred yards or so farther down, the world dropped away. A cloud of mist beyond sparkled subtle rainbows.

It was stark, strange and beautiful. Even better, the Jeep was maybe a hundred yards away, parked up on the bank. It looked intact and untouched. And it was on their side of the river.

"We caught a lucky break there," Matt said. "Let's hope it holds."

She looked up at him, and when their eyes met, her capable facade threatened to crack and crumble. It hadn't been that hard to hold it together while they were moving, but now, with their one real hope within reach, fear crowded close, tightening her chest and stealing her breath.

If they couldn't drive out in the Jeep, they couldn't warn the others that it wasn't just four or five hired thugs. Instead, they were dealing with a highly organized and well-armed camp. *Terrorists,* she thought. But she didn't say the word aloud, because regardless of who the militants worked for, they would be en route to the crash site, looking to confirm the kills. Which meant that the Jeep better damn well work.

"Hey." Matt dropped to a crouch, so they were at eye level. "You're doing great."

She nodded, gritting her teeth when they wanted to chatter, and forcing a smile that felt ghastly. "Don't worry. I've got your back."

"I know." Still holding his Sig Sauer in one hand, he used the other to catch the back of her neck and draw her in for a kiss.

Logic said the timing was totally wrong. But the kiss was exactly right.

The press of his lips steadied her. The touch of his tongue said *we're in this together.* The slant of his mouth

across hers reminded her that when it came to dangerous situations, they were batting a thousand. And the
warmth that rose in her, suffusing her body and lighten-
ing the heavy weight on her heart reminded her that she
was with a man who had always believed in protecting
others, even when he'd stopped believing in himself.
And she, who never ever leaned, let herself lean into
him for a precious second, drawing strength.

When they drew apart, he cupped her cheek in an un-
characteristically tender gesture. "No regrets, Gigi."

Remembering their lovemaking, she smiled slightly.
"No regrets."

"I love you."

Gigi froze. Heat slashed through her—maybe panic,
maybe exhilaration, maybe some of each—and her fingers went suddenly numb where they clutched her life-
lines, him on one side, her gun on the other. "I… Oh,
wow."

His grin was decidedly crooked, not an expression
she had seen on him before. It lightened him up despite
everything, making him look younger, more approach-
able, even a little roguish. Very much like a man a friend
would call "Blackie."

He took her gun hand and raised the Beretta between
them. "Cover me…partner."

Then he gave her hand a last squeeze and slipped past
her, staying low against the riverbank as she headed for
the Jeep.

She watched him go, staggered, her mind spinning.
It was just the moment, she told herself. He couldn't
possibly love her. It was too soon; they were too different; everything was fresh, shiny and new now, but when

that wore off the cracks would show. Opposites might attract, but they didn't stick for the long haul.

I love you, too. The words were trapped deep inside her, unsaid. She was entirely out of her depth. Love was too important to get wrong. How could she know for certain if it was going to last? She had thought she was in love before, and it had nearly destroyed her when it ended. Yet her feelings now were ten times stronger, a hundred. And as she watched Matt jump lightly from the concealment of the riverbank to the open ground above, her heart pounded with fear. Not for herself, this time, but for him. If anything happened to him… No, she wouldn't think it. Couldn't face it.

But it was that fear that broke her from her shocked paralysis and got her moving. Heart drumming lightly against her ribs, she edged farther along the riverbank, the rushing roar of the water and the deeper thunder of the falls covering the sound of her movement. She stayed concealed, but moved so she could see most of the clearing where the Jeep was parked. She covered her partner—her lover—as he headed for their best hope of surviving and warning the others what was happening inside the Forgotten.

And for the first time in her career, she wasn't fighting against something—crime, bloodshed, injustice— she was fighting *for* something.

Him. And, maybe, their future together.

MATT'S HEAD WAS CLEAR, his heart full, his senses attuned to his surroundings as he slipped between the Jeep and its rocky overhang. His cop self checked the frame and peeked through the windows, looking for evidence of a trap, while his ranger half listened for changes in the rhythms around him, the sudden silence that said predators were near.

No trap, no unwanted company, you're good to go. More, he was whole, connected, and entirely in the moment.

Becoming his better cop and ranger self hadn't been about blocking out his emotions after all, it seemed. He had needed to accept them instead, embrace them.

When he had headed off to France with Ian, he had been so full of a college hotshot's self-importance, so wrapped up in himself that he'd skipped his last visit home to go to a party being thrown by a guy he barely knew, to hit on a girl whose name he didn't remember. He hadn't told his parents he loved them, hadn't teased his sister one last time—he had thought there would be time for all that later, after Europe. After college. Whenever. But then they died and there hadn't been a later. There had only been grief, heartbreak, and raw, tearing regrets.

Not this time, he thought as he eased open the driver's-side door, took a quick look around, and then felt up underneath the overhanging section of dashboard where he and his rangers left their keys. Relief kicked when he found them right where they belonged. It looked like the Jeep had gone undetected, that they might be in the clear, after all. If he and Gigi could get back into radio range, he could mobilize a full-scale response. Not even Proudfoot could ignore the presence of an armed camp in his territory. And if the mayor tried to—if he was part of whatever was going on—Tucker, Fax and the others would go right over the top of him.

And damned if it didn't feel good knowing that he was part of a team like that.

Easing partway out from behind the Jeep, he flashed a sign toward where Gigi was hiding, then held up the keys. *Stay there, I'll come get you.* He was just easing back into concealment when there was a thump and a hiss from the nearby trees, and something came hurtling straight for him.

Incoming!

He flung himself away. Behind him, the missile slammed into the Jeep and detonated. In front of him was Gigi. He bolted toward her, and—

Shockwave. Searing heat.

Blackness.

THE IMAGES BURNED themselves onto Gigi's retinas: Matt's body silhouetted against the blast, his arms outstretched, his mouth shaping her name. Then, moments later, him lying crumpled on the ground, unmoving, the Jeep in flames behind him.

No! The scream reverberated in her head and pain ripped through her chest. Inwardly, she went fetal. Outwardly, though, she bolted along the riverbank, clutching the Beretta so hard her fingers numbed.

She sobbed silently as she ran, choking on grief and guilt. He'd trusted her to watch his back, but she hadn't seen or heard the grenade launcher, still didn't know exactly where the RPG had come from. One second, she was clandestinely giving him the thumbs-up for finding the keys, and the next... *Oh, God.*

"Please let him be okay," she whispered. Then, not caring if it was reckless or not, only knowing that she had to get to him, she vaulted onto the plateau and sped toward him, staying low, her mouth souring with fear.

He'd said he loved her. And she had frozen—not because she felt nothing, but because she didn't trust the huge, overwhelming feelings she had for him.

As he'd walked away, she told herself she needed time to think it through, time for the two of them to figure out if they could make it work. But even waiting five minutes had been too long.

She reached him, and had to choke back a sob. He lay facedown. His shirt was torn, his back streaked with blood, but she couldn't tell if it was still flowing, or even if he was breathing. Beyond him, the flames had died down to inky, foul-smelling smoke.

She crouched and moved to touch him with a shaking hand. "Matt? Can you hear—"

Movement blurred *above* her. Ambush!

She jerked back, gasping and bringing up the Beretta as a man leaped down from the rocky overhang. He landed on her with both feet, knocking her down and away. They rolled, grappling, and he nailed her with a vicious wrist chop that numbed her hand and sent her gun skidding. Then he was on her, straddling her, pinning her. She tried to knee him, but couldn't shift his heavy bulk, tried to twist away, but didn't have any leverage.

She was trapped. Oh, God. Terror rose, choking her.

Her dark-haired captor was wearing hunter's camouflage, a full suit of it that looked fresh out of the catalog, along with a utility belt that held a GPS, spare ammo for a shotgun she didn't see and a couple of fist-size canisters that were either grenades or gas.

His breath was hot on her face as he leaned over her, his blue eyes dark and feral. "You're in luck, bitch. The boss said to bring him a survivor, if there were any. He wants to know how much the cops have figured out."

A trickle of strength seeped into her and she sneered, "They know about everything. The camp, the stuff, all of it. If you want to get out of here, I'd do it now, because they'll be here any minute."

"Shut up." He backhanded her, the blow made heavy and hard by the pistol he had clenched in his fist.

Agony exploded in her jaw and her head whipped to the side. She cried out, not just in pain, but with the gut-deep wrongness of what was happening, and the horrible realization that Matt had been right—it was nothing like cardboard cutouts and training spars. Real blood ran from a cut on her cheek, real tears leaked from her eyes.

Her captor leaned in and rasped, "You'd better re-think that answer. You try lying to the boss and you'll wind up dead, too."

The word hit her harder than her attacker had. Dead? No, that was impossible. Matt couldn't be dead. He had just said he loved her. And she was supposed to have been watching his back.

She let out a single broken sob and turned her head away as her captor whipped off his belt and used it to lash her hands together behind her back, then sobbed again as he got to his feet and dragged her up by her bonds.

"Move." He shoved her ahead of him, then prodded

her with the Beretta. When they got closer to the line of strange, gnarled trees, she saw a battered military-style Jeep with no top or doors, and bare foam showing through tears in the upholstery.

She hadn't heard it. Even with the roaring noise of the water, she should have heard something, seen something.

"Get in." He shoved her in, pushing her back so her hands were trapped beneath her.

Her shoulders screamed, but that was nothing compared to the terrible, awful feeling that swept through her as she craned back and caught sight of Matt's body. Her heart cracked and bled; tears ran down her cheeks at the realization that she had waited too long, that in just a few short days he had gone from being adversary to lover, and now to loss.

And regret. Terrible, awful regret.

Chapter Seventeen

Groaning, Matt levered himself up and crouched for a second. His head spun and his ears rang, but that was nothing compared to the raw rage and hatred flowing through his veins, and the burning churn of the man he was becoming combined with the chill command of the one he used to be.

Gigi. Her name was a talisman, a focal point that got him on his feet.

He had regained consciousness too late to protect her, but he had heard where the bastard was taking her: back to the hidden campsite where, even if he could get through the perimeter, he would be one man against an army. It would be certain death for both of them.

Which meant he couldn't let them get to the campsite. He had to intercept them somehow. But the Jeep was toast and his Sig was gone, lost in the explosion. He was totally on his own.

Flashing back on the brief glimpse of things he had caught from the air, he headed for the waterfall. He forced his legs to carry him because there wasn't any alternative—no backup, no intel, no nothing—and failure wasn't an option.

His heart thudded in his chest. *Hang on, sweetheart. I'm coming.* Somehow.

The falls tumbled down from a wide, rocky promontory, fell four stories, and slammed into a pool that under normal circumstances was probably good and deep, but because of the drought looked churned-up and angry. No more than a half mile beyond it, though, the waterway spread out and became even shallower. And a single set of wet tire tracks emerged on one side, showing where the bastard had come through. There was no sign of him having gone the other way.

Matt's cop self said human beings were creatures of habit, which meant the guy would leave the way he had come in. The ranger in him said only an idiot would jump. Or a man in love.

Holding the image of gorgeous gray eyes snapping with mingled temper and arousal, and remembering what it felt like to lose himself inside her, wake up next to her, he backed away from the edge, took four running steps…and jumped.

GIGI'S SHOULDERS BURNED with every bump and rattle of the Jeep, her legs ached from bracing in the foot well as she struggled to free herself from her bonds. Her captor had threaded the seat belt through the leather strap so she couldn't launch herself out of the open-doored vehicle. The narrow edges of the leather belt cut into her hands and wrists, unyielding.

He held the Beretta trained on her as he drove.

Her mind swung violently from pure terror to calculating rage and back again. One moment she wanted to curl in a ball, the next she imagined herself breaking

free, grabbing her Beretta away from her captor, and
unloading it into his sneering face. He was no cardboard
cutout, but she could do it. Not just to escape, but for
Matt.

She pictured his face, his body, the way he moved,
the fierce light of determination in his eyes when he saw
something that needed to be done, and the way he was
always there for the people around him, even when he
seemed to be utterly disconnected from the world.

Oh, Matt. She wanted to close her eyes and pretend it
was all a nightmare. But she couldn't, because it wasn't.
This was really happening.

How arrogant she had been, how unrealistic to think
she could save other people from situations like this one.
She couldn't even save herself. What was more, she had
failed the man she loved.

Love. Yes, that was it.

Too late, she admitted to herself that she was in love
with him—she had started falling that very first moment
in the hallway, and had toppled cleanly over that night
in the safe house, when he'd imprinted himself indelibly
on her soul. And, too late, she understood where he had
been coming from, truly understood what he'd been
through as she felt the fear, anger, rage, impotence and
rending, tearing grief of losing him. She gave a shuddering sob and went limp.

The leather strap gave slightly.

Adrenaline flared through her, swerving her mind
back to revenge and the thin-seeming hope of escape.
Pulse pounding in her ears, she tugged experimentally.
Felt it give another fraction of an inch.

She had to relax and let it come, she realized; she

couldn't force it. And if that was supposed to be a life lesson from some higher power, she would deal with that particular epiphany later.

How much time did she have? Her heart raced as she made herself stay limp and worked one hand partway out of her bonds, little by precious little.

The Jeep broke through the old-man trees into a clearing near the same river they had been at before. Only it was shallower and wider here, downstream of the pounding waterfall. She held her breath when she caught sight of a rocky promontory halfway up: it was the one from Tanya's sketch, she was sure of it. But what did it mean? Was it a coincidence? A connection?

Gigi's grief didn't fade, but she could make herself think through it, using rage and regret to sharpen her senses as the driver muttered something under his breath, downshifted and gunned the vehicle into the river. Water sprayed up and in as the vehicle jolted and lurched. One of Gigi's feet slipped and she swung violently to the side with an involuntary gasp.

"Son of a—" Her captor took a hand off the wheel, grabbed her shirt and jerked her back upright. The wrench nearly yanked one shoulder out of its socket, but one wrist slipped from the wet leather. And she was free!

Still cursing, unaware that she had escaped her bonds, he fought the wheel, sliding on sprung upholstery made slick with the water that gushed over them as the four-wheeler went in deeper, bucking over the rocks.

Acting on rage and instinct, she screamed and launched herself onto her captor. She slammed a knee onto his gun hand and went for his throat, wrapping the leather around it and pulling as tightly as she could. She screamed again—a noise of hatred and heartbreak.

For a second, surprise gave her the upper hand. Then his foot came off the gas and he surged up against her, breaking her hold. He slammed an elbow into her jaw, knocking her back against the passenger's seat. Her head banged into the edge of the empty doorframe, and the world blurred.

He rose over her and aimed the Beretta point blank.

Everything came back into focus in that moment of blinding terror. She saw his cruel blue eyes, saw no remorse or pity, only a killer's calculation.

Panic slashed, emptying her mind.

"I'll talk," she blurted. "I'll tell your boss everything."

His eyes flashed. "Too late. I'll just tell him you were both dead when I got there." His finger tightened, the mechanism clicked—

A monstrous roar erupted from behind him as a figure lunged up, out of the water, grabbed him from behind and dragged him down. The gunman howled and his shot went wild, and then the gun flew free, landing in the driver's seat.

Gigi gaped as fire poured into her veins and her heart expanded in her chest. *"Matt!"*

His shirt was gone, his pants torn to the knee on one side, and blood streamed in the water that ran off his body, but he was there. He was alive!

Relief poured through her, pure and profound, but then her captor surged up, nearly tore away, and then spun back and kicked Matt in the stomach. He folded, the breath exploding from his lungs, and nearly went down.

She screamed and went for the gun.

The other man grabbed it a split second after she did, and they grappled for the weapon. She kicked at his face, caught him in the shoulder and made him howl. But then he twisted the gun free and fired.

Gigi threw herself backward out the far door.

"NO!" Matt exploded back out of the water and slammed into the gunman, driving them both against the side of the vehicle. He slammed the man's wrist against the doorframe, and there was a sickening crack. The man howled, and the Beretta went flying into the river.

"You. Don't. Touch. Her." Matt punctuated each of his words with a slamming blow that hammered his enemy into the river, until finally the man went limp, sprawled half into the driver's-side foot well, no longer a threat.

Once the guy was down, Matt yanked off his belt, cranked it around the guy's wrists and through the steering wheel, and pulled so tight that the guy's hands went white.

"Matt!" Gigi flew to him as he drew back his arm for another blow. At the sound of her voice, his head snapped up, his eyes locked onto her and his face flooded with all the same emotions that were suddenly filling her.

Relief made her sob, triumph made her smile and joy made her fling herself into his arms.

"Gigi." He caught her close, clamping on so tightly that she couldn't breathe. She didn't care, though. All

she cared about was the man holding her, murmuring her name. He shifted to kiss her lips, her face, her temple, then back to her lips again.

The kiss wasn't about seduction; it was about connection. She fused her mouth to his, poured herself into him and took his heat in return. Then she tore her lips away and said against his mouth, "I love you, too. I almost didn't get to say it. I love you. I love you. I think I started loving you that very first moment. Alyssa's right. There really is such a thing as love at first sight—and I'm in it."

His eyes burned green fire. "It's about time you admitted it. And people say *I'm* stubborn."

"What do you mean 'about time'?" Crazy exhilaration rose in her as she squared off opposite him. "It was like fifteen minutes. What if—" She broke off, new terror slashing through her at the sound of an incoming helicopter.

"Run!" He caught her hand and they bolted for the far bank. But the rocks beneath them shifted unsteadily and the water dragged at their legs.

They weren't going to make it.

A ROAR OF DENIAL BURNED Matt's throat, but he didn't have time to be pissed at the unfairness of the situation. His mind churned through hostage scenarios, negotiation tactics, something—anything—that would keep them alive. Because as long as they were alive and together, they had a fighting chance.

"Stay behind me." He stopped and turned as the rotor noise ratcheted up and his stomach sank at the realization that there was more than one chopper. Who were these people?

He braced himself squarely in front of Gigi, keeping a hand back, linked with hers to give her a reassuring squeeze. "I love you," he said over his shoulder.

Her eyes were wet and scared, but she smiled through trembling lips. "I love you, too. No regrets."

"No regrets." Because life wasn't about avoiding risk. It was about living in the present, and making each moment count.

The engine noise screamed and three choppers appeared downstream, flying low, in battle formation, weapons hot.

Gigi screamed in joy. "Look!"

The choppers were sleek, black and familiar, and wore tail numbers that didn't look quite right.

It wasn't the bad guys. It was backup.

"Hey!" He let go of her hand to wave his arms over his head. "Fax. *Hey!*"

The lead chopper roared directly over them while the other two peeled off and headed away, in the direction of the camouflaged camp. As the remaining chopper circled and headed for a landing on a small, rocky strip near the waterfall, Matt caught Gigi by the waist and swung her around. "We made it!"

She laughed and wrapped her arms around his neck, holding on as if she never intended to let go. Which was just fine with him.

The chopper settled down and the engine cut out. Moments later, the door opened and Fax and Chelsea emerged and headed straight for them. Another agent, this one wearing a pilot's headset, dropped down and headed for the Jeep, where the man they had captured had regained consciousness, and was furiously trying to escape from his bonds.

Matt and Gigi met Fax and Chelsea halfway, at the river's edge. "Thanks for the backup," Matt said. "Sorry about the chopper."

Fax winced. "That doesn't sound good."

Chelsea poked him in the ribs. "Don't listen to him. We were patched into your chopper's cameras and saw the whole thing. It gave us the leverage to mobilize agents up here as well as out to Sector Nine." She glanced from Matt to Gigi and back. "You guys both okay?"

"We'll live," Gigi said, glancing up at him. She threaded her fingers through his and squeezed, and it felt like she had just touched his heart.

They had things to work through, it was true, but after seeing her in the line of fire, he knew he couldn't keep her in the background. She was made for action, thrived on it. But at the same time, he saw a new awareness in her, and knew that the connection they had forged had brought home the realities of what it meant to knowingly walk into a critical situation. She would be more careful in the future…and she would have him to watch her back.

It was time for him to get back on the job. He didn't know what the next few months would hold for them—or for the investigation—but he knew that whatever they did, they would be doing it together.

He lifted their joined hands and pressed a kiss to her knuckles. "Yeah. We're going to be just fine."

* * * * *

HARLEQUIN
INTRIGUE

COMING NEXT MONTH

Available June 14, 2011

#1281 COWBOY BRIGADE
Daddy Corps
Elle James

#1282 LASSOED
Whitehorse, Montana: Chisholm Cattle Company
B.J. Daniels

#1283 BROKEN
Colby Agency: The New Equalizers
Debra Webb

#1284 THE MISSING TWIN
Guardian Angel Investigations: Lost and Found
Rita Herron

#1285 COOPER VENGEANCE
Cooper Justice: Cold Case Investigation
Paula Graves

#1286 CAPTURING THE COMMANDO
Colleen Thompson

HICNM0511

REQUEST YOUR FREE BOOKS!
2 FREE NOVELS PLUS 2 FREE GIFTS!

BREATHTAKING ROMANTIC SUSPENSE

YES! Please send me 2 FREE Harlequin Intrigue® novels and my 2 FREE gifts (gifts are worth about $10). After receiving them, if I don't wish to receive any more books, I can return the shipping statement marked "cancel." If I don't cancel, I will receive 6 brand-new novels every month and be billed just $4.24 per book in the U.S. or $4.99 per book in Canada. That's a saving of at least 15% off the cover price! It's quite a bargain! Shipping and handling is just 50¢ per book in the U.S. and 75¢ per book in Canada.* I understand that accepting the 2 free books and gifts places me under no obligation to buy anything. I can always return a shipment and cancel at any time. Even if I never buy another book, the two free books and gifts are mine to keep forever.

182/382 HDN FC5H

Name _____ (PLEASE PRINT)

Address _____ Apt. #

City _____ State/Prov. _____ Zip/Postal Code

Signature (if under 18, a parent or guardian must sign)

Mail to the **Reader Service:**
IN U.S.A.: P.O. Box 1867, Buffalo, NY 14240-1867
IN CANADA: P.O. Box 609, Fort Erie, Ontario L2A 5X3

Not valid for current subscribers to Harlequin Intrigue books.

**Are you a subscriber to Harlequin Intrigue books
and want to receive the larger-print edition?
Call 1-800-873-8635 or visit www.ReaderService.com.**

* Terms and prices subject to change without notice. Prices do not include applicable taxes. Sales tax applicable in N.Y. Canadian residents will be charged applicable taxes. Offer not valid in Quebec. This offer is limited to one order per household. All orders subject to credit approval. Credit or debit balances in a customer's account(s) may be offset by any other outstanding balance owed by or to the customer. Please allow 4 to 6 weeks for delivery. Offer available while quantities last.

Your Privacy—The Reader Service is committed to protecting your privacy. Our Privacy Policy is available online at www.ReaderService.com or upon request from the Reader Service.

We make a portion of our mailing list available to reputable third parties that offer products we believe may interest you. If you prefer that we not exchange your name with third parties, or if you wish to clarify or modify your communication preferences, please visit us at www.ReaderService.com/consumerschoice or write to us at Reader Service Preference Service, P.O. Box 9062, Buffalo, NY 14269. Include your complete name and address.

Harlequin® Blaze™ brings you
New York Times *and* USA TODAY *bestselling author*
Vicki Lewis Thompson with three new steamy titles
from the bestselling miniseries SONS OF CHANCE

Chance isn't just the last name of these rugged
Wyoming cowboys—it's their motto, too!

Read on for a sneak peek at the first title,
SHOULD'VE BEEN A COWBOY

Available June 2011 only from Harlequin® Blaze™.

"THANKS FOR NOT TURNING ON THE LIGHTS," Tyler said. "I'm a mess."

"Not in my book." Even in low light, Alex had a good view of her yellow shirt plastered to her body. It was all he could do not to reach for her, mud and all. But the next move needed to be hers, not his.

She slicked her wet hair back and squeezed some water out of the ends as she glanced upward. "I like the sound of the rain on a tin roof."

"Me, too."

She met his gaze briefly and looked away. "Where's the sink?"

"At the far end, beyond the last stall."

Tyler's running shoes squished as she walked down the aisle between the rows of stalls. She glanced sideways at Alex. "So how much of a cowboy are you these days? Do you ride the range and stuff?"

"I ride." He liked being able to say that. "Why?"

"Just wondered. Last summer, you were still a city boy. You even told me you weren't the cowboy type, but you're...different now."

He wasn't sure if that was a good thing or a bad thing. Maybe she preferred city boys to cowboys. "How am I different?"

"Well, you dress differently, and your hair's a little longer. Your face seems a little more chiseled, but maybe that's because of your hair. Also, there's something else, something harder to define, an attitude…"

"Are you saying I have an attitude?"

"Not in a bad way. It's more like a quiet confidence."

He was flattered, but still he had to laugh. "I just admitted a while ago that I have all kinds of doubts about this event tomorrow. That doesn't seem like quiet confidence to me."

"This isn't about your job, it's about…your…" She took a deep breath. "It's about your sex appeal, okay? I have no business talking about it, because it will only make me want to do things I shouldn't do." She started toward the end of the barn. "Now, where's that sink? We need to get cleaned up and go back to the house. Dinner is probably ready, and I—"

He spun her around and pulled her into his arms, mud and all. "Let's do those things." Then he kissed her, knowing that she would kiss him back, knowing that this time he would take that kiss where he wanted it to go. And she would let him.

Follow Tyler and Alex's wild adventures in
SHOULD'VE BEEN A COWBOY
Available June 2011 only from Harlequin® Blaze™
wherever books are sold.

Harlequin

SPECIAL EDITION

Life, Love and Family

LOVE CAN BE FOUND IN THE MOST UNLIKELY PLACES, ESPECIALLY WHEN YOU'RE NOT LOOKING FOR IT...

Failed marriages, broken families and disappointment. Cecilia and Brandon have both been unlucky in love and life and are ripe for an intervention. Good thing Brandon's mother happens to stumble upon this matchmaking project. But will Brandon be able to open his eyes and get away from his busy career to see that all he needs is right there in front of him?

FIND OUT IN

WHAT THE SINGLE DAD WANTS...

BY *USA TODAY* BESTSELLING AUTHOR

MARIE FERRARELLA

AVAILABLE IN JUNE 2011
WHEREVER BOOKS ARE SOLD.